JEZEBEL

AN ANGELS OF WAR NOVELLA

PREVIOUSLY IN THE SERIES:

Angels of War: Veritas
Angels of War: Talion

**GET READY FOR THE EPIC CONCLUSION TO
THE *ANGELS OF WAR* SERIES:**

Angels of War: Terminus

JEZEBEL

AN ANGELS OF WAR NOVELLA

A Novella by D.J. Thompson

www.masterlesspress.com

Masterless Press
www.masterlesspress.com

Jezebel: An Angels of War Novella
Copyright © 2019 by D.J. Thompson
Cover design by Hampton Lamoureux

First Masterless Press print edition: March 2019

Printed in the United States of America

ISBN: 978-1-7323064-0-0 (print)
ISBN: 978-1-7323064-5-5 (ebook)

AUTHOR'S NOTE

Welcome to the story of Isabella Monroe! This college girl is a raunchy, sassy, flirt who's not afraid use her *assets* to get what she wants, even in times of global upheaval and war … As such, this book contains some carnal, provocative themes that probably aren't suitable for younger audiences … Don't worry, there are no *50 Shades of Grey* scenes here, but she does dabble in some adult activities. Be advised.

Jezebel is a companion story to the *Angels of War* series that serves as a bridge between *Angels of War: Veritas* (Book 1) and *Angels of War: Talion* (Book 2). It can probably be read as a standalone, but the first seven chapters of *Jezebel* occur during Dion Johnson's story in *Veritas*. That means there are some **BIG** spoilers ahead … For the best reading experience, please give *Angels of War: Veritas* a read first and then dive on into this story! Chronologically, Isabella's story concludes early in *Talion*. So, if you want to go into the second book just as in the dark as Dion and the gang, you might want to finish the last six chapters [or the whole novella] after *Talion*, but it's not necessary.

Lastly, as stated in *Angels of War: Veritas*, this novella is set in a version of society where the conspiracies related to real-world events might actually be true. This is a work of fiction, and I believe conspiracy theories and other controversial topics are necessary ingredients for good storytelling when it comes to military fiction and thrillers. The conspiracies addressed in this book are not necessarily a reflection of my beliefs.

"You cannot make a man by standing a sheep on its hind-legs. But by standing a flock of sheep in that position you can make a crowd of men." – Sir Max Beerbohm

"None are more hopelessly enslaved than those who falsely believe they are free." – Goethe

PART ONE

THE TRUTH

1
SHAMELESS

March 15

WITH MY HIPS swinging side to side, I slowly bring my panties
down toward my knees. Now I shift onto my ass and pull those
undies off. I briefly caress my tits before my finger gets a mind of
its own and starts tracing a path south.

Ding. That's the sound of the first tip of the day.

College is too damn expensive. And my mom isn't exactly rich.
Hell, she's barely making it and she's too overwhelmed with
putting my sister Kirsten through medical school to worry about
helping me, the stoner majoring in psych ... So, I borrow what I
can from those goddamn scam artists who shell out loans like Bible
tracts and earn the rest of with my body, my innate ability to
seduce, and the internet.

My dream was to be a professional contemporary dancer, but
that's not the most lucrative career, and the odds of making it big
weren't really in my favor. After flaming out in the audition round
of *So You Think You Can Dance*, I decided to transition to modeling.
I've been featured in YouTube skits, work that isn't hard to find
here in Los Angeles, and in Instagram posts modeling clothes and
beauty products. But judging from the number of likes across the
web, most people have seen me shaking it on CollegiateCams.com
as Bella Roemon, a shitty pseudonym for Isabella Monroe that any

pornoholic with an above average IQ could probably figure out. Making money on an adult site doesn't bother me because I have no problem being naked in front of anyone. I love it, actually. There's something exhilarating about having people so entranced by my naked form that they get high off of endorphins and want to pay money just to see my goods. It's also a huge confidence booster. If I never put myself out there and had crowds of men drool and lust for me when I used to work the poles, I'd never know what it was like to be this free.

It was about a year ago, just after I turned nineteen, that a girl in my modern dance class told me how much she made as an exotic dancer. That's when I said screw graduating with student loan debt and started taking shifts at The Library, a strip club that's about a half-hour from campus. I'd been twerking and winding my hips on Instagram since my junior year of high school, so I already knew how to be sexy for an audience; though it was different when the audience was watching me live. It took a few nights for me to shake the nervousness. The private dances, however, were no biggie for me. I might be an extrovert, but some things are just easier one on one. And I am damn good at sex, which made me spec-fucking-tacular at lap dances.

Stripping didn't last long, though. There are lines that I'm not willing to cross, and my clientele were more than willing to cross them without my consent. Maybe at a better place the bouncers would have stepped in, but I'm not afraid to look out for myself the way my dad taught me to, and after a few situations where I had to crotch-punch or slap some handsy bastards, they threatened to fire my ass. I quit before that happened and I was back working part-time as a waitress.

Fun fact: I like porn. Girl-girl, guy-on-girl, solo stuff—it doesn't matter. I watch it by myself on those lonely nights, I've watched with past boyfriends, with friends-with-benefits. So when the bills started piling up again, I ordered a webcam on Prime.

At the end of tonight's show, I sit up and blow a kiss to the camera before cutting the feed. In a few clicks, I'm at the hosting site's dashboard to check tonight's earnings. $844 in tips, plus some gifts from my Amazon wish list—not bad, not bad at all. In two nights, I've made enough for rent, groceries, some shopping, and a couple hundred bucks toward that trip to Hawaii I've been dreaming of.

Satisfied, I close my laptop and my eye catches the picture of my father and an eight-year-old me on the dresser. The guilt hits me in the chest the way it always does.

Daddy, I really hope there isn't a heaven where you can watch me from above …

After a shower, I pull my honey brown curls into a ponytail then I spend almost an hour on makeup. Once I'm all done, I slip on a low-cut, burgundy top, a black skirt, heels, spritz some perfume on my neck then it's time to head out.

"Hey Izzy, you see this shit?" Nicki asks as I walk into our living room.

"Nah, I don't like action movies," I say, rifling through my bag in search of my fake I.D.

"This isn't a movie! It's the goddamn news!"

I stop and look at the TV. A scene from London shows people tearing each other apart, literally tearing off flesh with their hands and mouths. The next scene shows a brawl going down outside of a gigantic palace. The announcer says that similar riots are taking place in major cities from Europe to Japan.

"Holy shit!" I say. "I guess that prick in the Star Wars helmet meant what he said the other night ..." I start toward the door, my heels clopping against wood.

"Wait, are you still going out?" Nicki asks.

"Uh, damn right I am. DJ TyDie got me into that big rooftop party tonight!"

"But they're saying America will be hit next!"

I make a farting sound with my mouth. "Well, if we're all going to die, I'd rather go out having fun than watching TV like somebody's grandma. Don't wait up, okay?"

March 16

It's like seven in the morning by the time I wake up. Chase is still fast asleep, snoring like a goddamn bear. I need to get out before he gets up and starts whining for me to spend the day with him. He's been getting annoying lately, bugging me about being together when he knows I want to be single after my last relationship, my first serious relationship, blew my life up. On weekends when I stay in the city, I usually crash at my best friend Riley's place, but after the fifth shot of tequila, the drunk, horny alter ego of mine that everyone calls Bella had to flirt with him over Snapchat and invite him out to the rooftop party I was at ...

I quietly get dressed and slip out of his apartment with my shoes in hand. The elevator is busted so I clop my way downstairs. As I reach the lobby, I see a gray Honda Civic pull up outside.

"You Isabella?" the driver asks as I step onto the sidewalk.

I check the app to make sure he's the right guy. Yup, and he looks even better in person. "That's me, Austin!" I say, grabbing the rear door handle.

"I dig your accent! Where are you from?"

"Texas. Grew up in Austin."

"Awesomeness! I'd live there if my name wasn't the same as the town …" He laughs, shifting the car into drive. "What brings you out here? You a model?"

"Something like that," I say.

"Sweet." His eyes look me over via the rearview mirror. "You had a good time last night?" He palms his face. "I'm sorry, that didn't come out right."

"Relax, hon," I say, patting his shoulder. "I did have a good time. Thanks for asking. "My crotch is kind of sore, though. Last night was a bit of a marathon, if ya know what I mean!"

His face goes beet red. "Uh, sure." He clears his throat then silence follows. "Do you mind if I play an audiobook?"

"Go on ahead."

We're bound for Riley's place in Pasadena. As he listens to some *Game of Thrones* bullshit, I scroll through Instagram on my dying phone. The site's flooded with videos and pictures of shit from overseas. Buildings on fire. Uncensored bodies sprawled in the streets. There's footage from a model I follow filming British soldiers shooting at people in the streets outside of her apartment. It all makes me a little anxious.

The driver slams on the damn brakes. The tires screech and we swerve right. He kills the radio. The only thing I hear are sirens, which is nothing out of the ordinary in this city.

"Something wrong?" I ask, eyeing the gridlock ahead. *Fucking LA traffic.*

"I thought I heard—"

He's cut off by the chatter of what sounds like gunfire. It actually sounds like the shootout I just watched on my phone. Something automatic, like the AR-15s my dad and I would fire at the range. A ground-shaking boom erupts behind us that damn near makes me piss myself. There are more screeching tires and then something hits the rear of our car, hard.

2
THE ANNEX

March 16

MY HEAD SLAMS into the back of the passenger seat and my phone flies out of my hand.

"The fuck …?" I mutter.

"You okay?" Austin asks.

Rubbing my forehead, I look back at the drop-top Audi that rear-ended us. The driver isn't moving. I'm pretty sure there are bullet holes in the rear panel. "Yeah, I'm peachy."

There are more gunshots. They sound closer than before. My heart starts thumping in my chest when I realize what's happening.

Austin gets out of the car then opens the door for me, extending a hand. "Come on! We need to get out here." He's barely audible over the encroaching sirens.

"Wait! My phone!" I dive back into the car and start feeling around under the seat for my iPhone with my shaky-ass hand. I palm it the second he tugs me along.

Austin leads me through the snarled traffic as something explodes behind us. Thanks to my dance training, I'm more agile in heels than most people are in sneakers. But even still, I struggle to keep up. The gunshots, the screams, the horns, the sporadic explosions—I'm so disoriented, I don't know where I am. Somewhere downtown, I think. I look back again to see an enraged mob swarming toward us, chewing up those behind us like a swarm of locusts. I stare longer than I should and I fucking trip, scraping my knee and hand. Some people are randomly beating on car hoods and windows. One guy bludgeons a woman with a pipe. When she puts up her hands to defend herself, he bites off her fingers and then starts chomping on her forearm. When Austin comes back and tries to pull me forward, I stand there, frozen, staring at some hipster getting stabbed to death by a cop. A few feet away is a massive brawl. Across the street, an older woman is gunned down by an Asian dude. Screams of terror and of rage are interspersed with laughter in the mob. I watch it all, fingernails involuntarily digging into Austin's arm.

What the fuck is happening!

My first thought is a zombie apocalypse, like in that old movie *28 Days Later*. Then I remember the guy in the helmet and the gas he was spreading around Europe and Asia. Apparently, he'd made it to LA too.

Those exposed begin exhibiting symptoms resembling clinical psychosis, they'd said on the CNN video I watched on Facebook a few minutes ago. The symptoms of Psycho Nerve Agent exposure I remember are an inability to reason and nervousness followed by rage and violent behavior ...

"We're under attack ..." I mutter to myself.

"Huh?" Austin grunts.

"This is a nerve gas attack!" I say a little louder.

A man covered in blood locks eyes with me and charges, bellowing out an incoherent mélange of pain, laughter, and anger. I know I should run but my body won't cooperate.

"Come on!" Austin says, yanking me back.

I kick off my heels and follow him as we run down an entrance ramp and duck into a vintage clothing store. My bare feet clap against the sticky floor on the way to the register where a girl and a guy are peeking over the counter. Something I stepped on along the way leaves a dull pain in my left foot, reminding me that I'll need shoes before I cripple myself and get mauled. I pull down a half-dozen shoeboxes listing my size and slip on a pair of white sneakers with red hearts all over them. Meanwhile, Austin is bracing himself against the front door as the madman punches the glass with bloody knuckles. The two retail workers have come around the counter and are dragging over display racks to blockade the door. Glass shatters and a bleeding arm bursts through and the man's large hand grabs Austin by the throat. The clerks scamper backward and watch in horror as a wild-eyed obese woman blasts into the store, snapping the madman's elbow as she knocks him to the floor. The woman charges at the clerks, pounces on the guy, and starts wailing on him. The female clerk throws herself over the counter and crashes into something out of sight. The first psycho howls in pain and/or rage as he starts punching Austin with the arm that works.

Dad raised you to be a fighter, I think while looking around for a weapon of some kind. Against the wall to my left is one of those poles with the hook you use to get out of reach clothes so I dart to it. I grab it and run back to the door as the dangly armed man grabs a glass shard and plunges it toward Austin, who grabs the man's arm with both hands. I aim for the bastard's chin and swing the pole like I'm Tiger Woods. He pulls back just in time to lose an eye as the hook end claws through the socket. I beat him over the head until the pole breaks, then I stomp on his skull with my heart-spotted sneakers. He stops moving, and my vision clears to see that I gouged out one of his eyes. A wave of nausea hits and I double over, puking too quickly for me to pull my hair out of the way.

"Behind you!" Austin says. He grabs the pole from me and dispatches the other nutjob barreling toward me with one hard swing.

"Are you okay, Tim?" the female clerk asks her coworker who has blood pouring down from his hairline.

"What does it fucking look like?" he snaps

Austin helps me up. "We need to get out of the city!"

"No shit," I say, harsher than I meant to.

A herd of psychos gathers outside the door as Austin drags me to cover. The last thing I see is a woman with her face pressed against the storefront window while screaming at a mannequin.

"There's a rear exit …" Tim groans as the girl ties a shirt around his scalp.

The glass and racks rattle as helicopters fly overhead. The two clerks lead us through the back of the store to an alley. A few people run by as we exit and Austin raises a metal bar that he pried from one of the display racks. They don't seem mad like the rest, just terrified. Since it seems they're running from danger, we follow them like herd animals.

Explosions rock the city from different directions and the frequency of gunshots increases as the gap between the gunfire and us shrinks. After decades of exporting it to dozens of countries around the world, war has finally come to America.

Austin leads the pack, but I'm right behind him, fighting the urge to bolt past him—if something jumps out in front of us, I'd rather it takes him instead of me. Like any good Texan, I was raised on brisket, but I exercise often enough to keep my heart and body in shape so it's easy to keep up.

Cops and SWAT teams stationed in the buildings above us lay down automatic rifle fire on the berserkers behind us. Some of the people they're killing are wearing police uniforms as well, which is blowing my mind. An explosion a few blocks down sends a cloud of dust barreling down the street, leaving us coughing and sooty like 9/11 victims.

We hit an intersection where military trucks roll up and let out soldiers in white, gray, and black camouflage. Instinctively, me and the group—Austin, the clothing store crew, and a few others who fell in along the way—double back and turn down an alley, then crouch behind a dumpster.

I plug my portable charger into my phone before that one percent hits zero. I call 911 but the circuits are jammed. This goddamn phone can't get a call out to anybody in my contact list either. I text Chase with trembling hands, asking him for help. I copy and paste the message to Riley, Nicki, and several other friends, then text my mom and sister to let them know I'm okay. I ask if they're okay because I don't know if it's just LA that's under attack or the whole friggin' country. Some messages fail to send. Some get through but responses don't follow.

Something mechanical rumbles in the distance. It grows closer and louder as the seconds pass.

"That's a goddamn tank," the guy next to me says. His white linen suit is torn and filthy and he's fondling a pistol that he must have picked up along the way. Sure enough, a gray behemoth grinds down the street in front of us.

"There's no way out," says the girl from the clothing store. Pretty sure Bethany was what I saw on her nametag.

"Our best chance might be to hunker down here until the National Guard comes through," the dude in the suit says.

"Yeah, fuck that," I say. "There are crazies everywhere, a tank roaming the streets, and cops mowing down people. When the army gets here, that'll be just another set of guns. You ever hear of collateral damage, dipshit?" I turn to Austin. "You gonna earn that

fare or not, hot stuff?" I make sure to bat my lashes and smile
pitifully.

He smiles. "Yeah, if you give me a five-star review."

"Deal. And a cold beer as a tip."

Austin looks at the others. "You guys coming with?"

The store workers nod hesitantly.

The dude in the linen suit shrugs. "Sure, until something better
comes along."

Austin slinks around the dumpster and crouch-walks to the
corner. When he waves us on that it's all clear, we follow him back
out to the main road, keeping low and moving behind cars. It takes
forever to advance two blocks. Military vehicles are continually
racing by so we are forced to keep hiding and waiting.

"Look!" Austin whispers, pointing at the intersection ahead.
"There's a police van."

Its red and blue lights are flashing. The passenger door is open
and there's a person slumped over in the seat. He's probably dead
like the guy marinating in a pool of blood by the rear bumper.
There are a few bullet holes in the doors but the tires don't look
flat. It looks promising.

The gunfire, the bomb blasts, engines—they all seem far off.
"Sounds like it's clear," I whisper.

"Let's go!" Austin says.

We scurry toward the van, moving quicker now. After tossing
the dead cop out, Austin scrambles through the passenger door
and over into the driver's seat. As I'm about to climb in behind
him, rumbling engines that grow louder by the second make me
pause. My head whips around and I see a caravan of armored
trucks speeding toward us. Some are black, some are gray. Two
green transport trucks with canvas tops follow them. A man in a

gray trench coat and a black helmet with a filtration system jutting out of it is aiming at us from the roof hatch of the lead vehicle.

I'm the first to put my hands up.

"Out of the vehicle!" the gunner shouts. The side door of his truck rattles open and a pair of soldiers advance on us while peering through the scopes of their rifles. One is wearing a gray trench coat and the other's in camouflage with a blinking belt.

The store clerks raise their hands. Austin raises his and slowly crawls out of the van. But the asshole in the stained linen suit decides to start waving his fucking gun around.

"Drop that fucking weapon!" the trench-coated man orders. He's wearing an American flag patch on his left arm.

"Don't be a fucking idiot," I hiss. "You'll get us all killed."

He doesn't listen, turning the pistol from the dude in the camouflage to the dude in the trench coat and back again with a trembling arm.

"Maybe you get a shot off," the trench coat says. "If you do, we've got ten more guns that'll light you up. But we don't want to shoot anyone. The Annex—this war we're fighting—is to save people, not kill them in cold blood."

"Oh really?" the suit spits. "And what about those people who went crazy after you attacked them with chemical weapons?"

"Unfortunately, they were necessary casualties sacrificed for the greater good. Like you." A shot cracks off and the suit's head snaps back as blood, brains, and bone spray out the back of his skull. A good deal of it lands on me.

The girl from the clothing store screams. So does the dude in the glasses who'd joined us with Mr. Suit. I drop to my knees, hands still raised. I'm sobbing and drooling like an idiot because I'm afraid I'll swallow some of the brains that I'm pretty sure splashed into my open mouth.

"Everyone down like Miss America here, hands behind your backs!" the trench coat barks. "Comply and no harm will come to you! That is a promise! We're here to help make your world a better place."

The camouflaged soldier forces my arms behind my back and zip-cuffs me. That's not a new experience for me—protesting the kleptocracy's despoiling of our society and our climate doesn't endear you to the pigs who defend their draconian laws. The key is not to panic and not resist.

"We're here to save you from corruption and from a government who wants you all sick, dead, or enslaved!" the trench coat says. "Cooperate and thrive! Resist and perish!"

The soldier lifts me up, and when I don't move, he shoves me. Hard. "Move it, princess."

3
SHEEPLE

March 16

MY BODY ROCKS and my head bobbles as the truck we're all crammed in rolls into potholes and over debris … some of it squishier than my stomach would like it to be. Clumped strands of hair are draped over my face, swaying back and forth before my unblinking eyes. The image of those before me flickers behind those filthy locks. They aren't from our group. There's a trio of hippie looking burnouts around my age, and an older couple. They're as much in shock as we are, but less filthy. Austin is right next to me. The dollar store clerks Tim and Bethany are all the way in the back.

I keep picturing all the things I've seen today—the corpses, the people getting stabbed and beaten to death. The guy I probably murdered. I eye the soldier sitting at the rear who's looking my way and wonder whether I was lucky to have been captured instead of killed. I can't imagine the horrible things they'll do to us once they get us to where we're going.

The sounds of war fade over time. Maybe forty minutes in, it's all quiet. Maybe an hour after that, we start slowing down. It's like there wasn't any traffic. Maybe they blocked off the roads before all hell broke loose, trapping everyone in the city.

The breaks squeal as our transportation comes to a jerking stop. The canvas parts and light floods in, blinding me. "Everyone out, one at a time," the trench coat orders.

I'm the sixth one out, right behind Austin. *Well, shit ...* They've brought us to the campus of California State University—San Bernardino, my very own college. Our group is forced into a single file line and herded like sheep toward a checkpoint at a fence that wasn't here when I left after class Friday.

Lines of refugees from other trucks on spill out, and we all converge into a mass. I try to keep up with Austin but the bastards on either side of me keep knocking into my shoulders like there's a free buffet at the end of this chaos. I whisper his name. He stops and grabs my elbow. He seems like a good guy. Sure, he's probably only going out of his way for me because he's hoping to get laid, but I really don't care about his motives right now. Until I come across people I know, he's all I've got.

Eventually, we're funneled back into a narrow line bound for a table manned by a bitchy Hispanic woman with a Mexican flag patch on the left sleeve of her trench coat. She starts us through a process degrading enough to make the TSA jealous: a full-body pat-down that relieves everyone of their wallets and other belongings before the zip-cuffs are snipped. For those ahead who have licenses, their IDs are scanned and a wristband is strapped around their wrists.

"Name?" the woman snaps.

"Isabella," I answer, voice wavering. "Isabella Monroe."

"Birth date and address?"

I tell her.

She types my info into the computer, scans a wristband, then straps it around my wrist. At the gate, another trench-coated woman frisks every inch of me, which seems pointless considering

Austin is being forced to strip down to his underwear like those ahead were. Demoralization tactics, I assume.

The strip club was a creepy place sometimes, but nothing like this. I notice a few male soldiers ogling me and I cover my chest for the first time in years. I'm grateful that I found my thong before I left this morning, but it's not like it's covering much …

Austin flinches as he is hosed down. Then he's shoved toward the next station. Now it's my turn. The cold blast power-washes me like I'm a car as I turn with my arms up, as instructed. When the stream hits my face, it gets in my nose and mouth, and I start coughing. It feels like I'm drowning and I panic a little.

I'm still coughing as I'm shoved to the station where clothes are being handed out. Squinting from burning, soapy eyes, I shuffle up to the man in gray who asks me what size shoes and clothes I need. I get a pair of black knockoff Crocs and a size small burgundy jumpsuit. *Well, at least it's my favorite color*, I think, trying to be positive.

I clutch the clothes to my chest, drying my eyes with the sleeve and walk barefoot across the hot cement, frantically looking around for Austin. The terrorists are filtering our group into two lines— those in the primes of our lives to the left and the young, old, sick, and injured to the right. Some people shout and struggle as they're separated from the people they came in with, but they're quickly pulled away. Some are tased into submission when our captors see the need or, I dunno, decide that a little brutality would be fun.

"Austin!" I call out, moving faster toward the pack. I stand there looking around for almost a minute but I can't find him. Anxiety is setting in. "Austin?" I call a little louder.

"Isabella!" he calls from somewhere ahead. A hand rises above the crowd and his face appears.

"Back in line!" a tall, stocky gray coat barks, shocking Austin's wet ribs with a cattle prod.

Austin falls, dropping his clothes and shoes.

"Austin!" I shout, running to him.

Some pretty boy in a gray trench grabs me by the arm. "Back of the line for you, Victoria Secret."

"I just need to get to my friend!" Austin begs. "Just let me get to her."

Tall-Gray grabs Austin by the hair and arm then lifts him onto his feet. "Pick up your shit and get your ass back where you were. Your friend will be fine if she follows the rules."

Austin turns back to me as I am shoved in line. "Please, let—"

"Follow instructions before I have to shock your ass!" the gray shouts, shoving him back into the flock.

At the west end of campus, we're ordered to get dressed. Then we're funneled into Jack H. Brown Hall and broken up into smaller groups before being herded into one of the lecture halls. I take a seat near the front as the rows behind me fill up one by one. An Asian woman dressed in gray stands behind the podium, a rifle slung across her back.

"Greetings," she begins. "On behalf of the Deciders, I'd like to offer my apologies for what we put you through today. Chaos and hysteria were necessary to destabilize those in control." She touches something on the podium and the projector displays a white, gray, and burgundy flag of a globe in the palm of a hand. "I am Susan Kwon. Those dressed in the uniforms I'm wearing are known as Loyals. We Deciders—the Deciders of Humanity—hail from every corner of the globe.

"Our mission is to bring forth the unification of the human race through the eradication of provincial governments and their armies. We are sworn enemies of the divisive constructs of religion, terrorism, ideology, and bigotry."

The screen switches to a portrait of some trust fund frat boy, maybe a little older than me, who's dressed in all white. "Carrying out the work of the founder, the Architect Richard Thomas, we Deciders are determined to create a new world order based on the vision of his brother, Ryan 'Maverick' Thomas. Regretfully, Ryan Thomas was assassinated by the U.S. after compiling Veritas, a collection of the war crimes, conspiracies, cover-ups, inhumane experiments, assassinations, and plans to reduce and enslave the population hatched by the elites dominating the world."

The screen changes again, showing Richard with a stunning-looking woman with glossy black hair and blue eyes, a jacked black guy, another preppy-looking asshole, and a guy who looked like a he was in a rock band.

"Using Veritas," Kwon continues, "Richard and longtime friends Tyrone Jones, Christopher Hawthorne, and Donald Chambers, along with his lover, Anne Buckingham, traveled the world, working in the shadows to expose the truth to thousands of soldiers and civilians and rallying us to join his ranks. Those people became the Loyals.

"You have been brought here today so we can teach you why the world you know is a lie. We will show you the truth—including the plans your government had to kill seventy percent of the population."

A map of UC San Bernardino's campus appears on the screen. "But before we can show you the truth, we need your help fortifying this campus against the minions of the old guard. You will be fed and given shelter during the time of your labor. And when the work is completed, you will be enlightened. Once you receive the knowledge contained in Veritas, you will be given a chance to join our movement. But more on that later …"

Fence and barricade duty—that's what my group is assigned to. As we file outside, I examine the cuts on my left hand.

"Hey," I say to the light-skinned black guy in all gray who's herding my part of the line. "Excuse me!"

He turns. "What do you want?"

I show him my palm and make a pitiful face. "Um, could I maybe get some antibiotics and some band-aids before I start working?" I brush the curls out of my face. "And maybe a bottle of water? Pretty please? You'd be my favorite person here."

His eyes search me over. "Sure, why not?" He escorts me to a tent where another gray is dragging crates out of a truck. "Yo, Bradshaw!"

"Sup, Shon?" he asks, dropping a crate into the dust.

"This one needs first aid. And some water."

The second soldier looks through his sunglasses at me. "Pretty sure Lieutenant Holt told us not to play favorites." He rummages through a container. "Especially not with potential *distractions*." He produces a first aid pouch and tosses it over. "Water's in the crate over there."

"It ain't like that, Bradshaw," my guard says. "She can't work if she's hurt and dehydrated." He hands me the first-aid kit. "Do what you need to do."

"Thanks," I say. I retrieve a bottle of water then hike up my pants and rinse my knee and hand before applying the ointment and bandages. Then I chug the rest of the warm water.

"You good?" Shon asks.

"Mhm!" I say, eyeing his chest patch. "Thanks so much, Corporal Anderson."

"No more favors for you until you earn them, you understand?"

I give him an ironic salute. "Oh, yes, sir. I'll be sure to put in some good work for my boys in gray."

That earns me a half-hearted shove toward my fellow worker ants as they dig a trench in the desert sun, their first down payment on our promised enlightenment. "Get to work," Anderson says. "I'll be keeping my eyes on you."

"I'll bet," I say, swaying my hips as I walk away. I see them both staring in the reflection of the armored truck's windshield.

So far, we've spent two hours fortifying the western end of campus. The entire time I've been left thinking about what Kwon told us—things I've suspected to be true for years.

Back in high school, a lot of shit went down in my life. It all started my freshman year when my dad died four months after being diagnosed with Stage III blood cancer and Stage IV lung cancer. His guess is he was exposed to something during his time as a soldier in the Gulf War.

After some bullshit with my dad's military pension, we lost our house. The apartment we moved to was in a different school district. I ditched my bubbly cheerleader persona and fell in with a bunch of stoners who talked conspiracies day in and day out. The shit they used to talk about reminded me of things my dad used to say, like:

You know the government's spying on us through our phones ...

The army hasn't "defended our freedom" since Grant and Sherman gave those Confederates the business in the Civil War. All they do now is keep the shipping lanes open for Wal-Mart and the House of Saud ...

The only reason we're in the Middle East is to set up shop there so we can have a strategic holding around Russia. You watch, we'll be gunning for Syria and Iran soon enough.

They're using the media to divide us politically and through a racial conflict. The whites will be fighting blacks and the liberals will be at war with the right. While we're busy killing our own, it'll allow the powers that be to catch us with our pants down.

The terrorists we're fighting today we've funded back in the day. Hell, we're still funding those towel heads …

After spending time with my band of conspiracy theorists, after listening to all of the podcasts they introduced me to, I began believing that the reason my dad got cancer was because of all the shit our government allows to be in food and drinks. I believed they wanted us all sick so their corporate overlords could rape our bank accounts before they thinned the herd with disease and drugs. I understood that college was a scam to keep us as financial debt slaves. I knew everything that happened in American news was either a means to expand power overseas or to rid the American people of their guns and civil liberties. It was obvious that both political parties were just two heads of the same beast that are put in power to achieve specific objectives and narratives while keeping us at odds. And the news? They were just propaganda engines used to keep the people misinformed, divided, and docile. And anyone who didn't believe those things were sheeple.

Depleted uranium in my father's ammunition gave him cancer? Sure. GMOs are a Trojan horse for Monsanto to enslave the world's farmers while systematically fucking up our health? You bet. Guaranteed profits and legal immunity for hedge fund bankers who donate equally to both parties? String them up. Ballooning tuitions to make us buckle under to management instead of unionizing and demanding our share of the pie? Not if I could help it. After meeting some activists during my second semester of college, I joined their club and we protested everything from police brutality to the Federal Reserve.

What these Deciders did makes me queasy, but isn't this the revolution we wanted all along? You can't overthrow a global elite without bloodshed. From what I've heard being whispered by the Decider soldiers, they're fighting in California, Seattle, Vegas, and Phoenix. Despite burning the world to the ground, I need to know what they know. I want proof that it's true. And if it is, I don't have any reason to be broken up about it. It sucks people are dying, and I hope my loved ones will be alright, but if the contents of Veritas are true, the real bad guys have been running the world the entire time.

4
DECIDER BY NATURE

March 18

TODAY IS OUR first day off. Not that I worked all that much over the past few days. I didn't work at all, really. I made nice with Sergeant Bradshaw and Corporal Anderson—or Owen and Shon, as we're on a first-name basis now—by talking conspiracy theories with them, prompting Owen to pull me from the work line so he could "better evaluate me." I reciprocated with a bit of flirting—a few light touches on the arm, some suggestive banter—enough to keep me on his good side without making him want to drag me into a dark corner somewhere. He's hot, and funny, and smart, so I'm not sure that'd be a bad thing, honestly. Ugh, there's just something about a man in uniform …

There are three knocks at the door then it creaks open. "Time for class," Joe, the chubby Loyal who works our floor announces.

My roommate Brie and I grab our copies of Veritas and follow him out. The soldiers escort my floor from our sleeping quarters in Serrano Village, the on-campus housing where I lived as a freshman.

While I walk, I flip through the book to where we left off with yesterday: the origin of the Federal Reserve on Jekyll Island, how megabanks and elites chose which political figures to put in power, and how they manipulated nations in order to steer the world to the endgame that they wanted. Previous classes covered depopulation plans and false flags used to start wars or infiltrate nations. It's all backed up by signed top-secret files and video confessions by government officials recently captured during the Annex. At this point, President Harry Odom himself wouldn't need to come to class and admit Veritas is the real deal. I already know everything I've ever suspected is true. The real enemy isn't the Deciders, it's the governments and elites of the world and, now more than ever, I want them all to go down.

Today's lesson will be on the pharmaceutical industry and how the true causes of certain diseases and their cures were suppressed from the public. I skimmed ahead last night before bed and learned some heavy shit: for one, that the weed extract CBD can prevent cancer and cure epilepsy and anxiety—reasons why it was probably illegal in the first place. I also saw something about the cure for Alzheimer's being suppressed by some lab in Pennsylvania, which sucks because I had to watch my favorite aunt suffer from that before she wandered off in the desert one summer in Texas and died … I imagine I'll be leaving class even more pissed off than before.

I load a tray of scrambled eggs, fruit, and oatmeal in the cafeteria and follow Brie to where the rest of our "friends" are sitting. I'm an extrovert by nature, and it was a lot easier to branch out and meet some people after seeing how cool and down to earth Owen and Shon are. Hell, the Deciders even gave us coffee and a bomb-ass hot meal after our first day working on the fence. Despite some rebellious types from the age thirty-five and up camp that I saw get roughed up for disobedience, the Deciders treated everyone else well and with respect.

My clique includes this frat boy from Kappa Sigma named Jason Dunn who I had a psych class with last semester, Bethany and Slim Tim from the clothing store, and a few other teens and twentysomethings. All of us are all pretty pro-Decider, or at least they claim to be. Better to be building a fence than waiting for the government to mow us down, I suppose. And it helps that they're working to find our family members at the other camps.

"Isabella? Isabella!"

I turn around and see Austin hurrying toward me with his tray. He sets it down and we hug.

"You're okay!" he says.

I laugh. "Of course, why wouldn't I be?"

He frowns and looks around. "Are you joking?"

"Dude, wake up. The world is a shitty place. These people are probably our only chance to fix it."

"Even if that is true, I'm getting out of here," he whispers into my ear. "There are a few of us who are planning an escape. I promised I'd get you home, so …"

"That's real sweet of you, but I don't want out. And you'll just end up getting yourself killed if you try, hon."

"I hear they're torturing the older folks on the other side. And I don't want to stick around to find out what they have planned for us."

"Izzy," Brie calls, "if we're late, we won't get good seats for the show!"

"Geez, give me a sec here."

"Uh, what show?" Austin asks.

I scowl. "Where have you been? The Deciders are taking down the capital of corruption and it's gonna be broadcasted in class today."

"The capital of corr—"

"DC, dude! They're blitzing DC today!"

Austin looks at me like I'm crazy. "Isabella—"

I pull him in for a hug. "The Deciders are waging war in all fifty states and in every country in the world," I whisper in his ear. "There's nothing for you out there. Stay here with me. Open your mind and try to see the truth. If you don't agree with what you find out, just pretend to blend in and keep your head down. Okay?"

"Yeah. Maybe you're right."

"I'm always right. Now let's eat."

March 22

At the end of the final Veritas class, we're led outside and instructed to line up at the trailer or tent that corresponds with the first letter of our last names. The L-M-N group gathers outside of a trailer on the lawn near the library.

"Looks like I'm over there," I say. "What's your last name again?"

"Lahey," Austin says.

"Ugh, I can't get rid of you!" I say, giving him a playful shove.

"If you wanted to get rid of me, you should have let me escape."

"Yeah, but then you'd be dead like your friends." I say, thinking back to the failed escape. Two Deciders were killed—one Loyal and a Vanguard, the subordinates in camouflage who are forced to fight for the Deciders' cause. I saw one of the shooters get shredded by the response team. I heard that a sniper took down the other. The bloody-faced escapees they caught were hauled past my group. I'm still not sure what happened to them.

Armed Loyals in those black, gas-filtering Deva helmets patrol up and down the line while we wait. Things were starting to get more lax around campus until those idiots tried breaking out. Now the Deciders are treating us like the new people they bring in on buses and sequester on the east end.

The line moves slower than one at the DMV but it's a nice evening and I'm in good company, so it isn't all bad. Austin's chatting away, looking at me all googly-eyed like a pubescent boy just noticing how hot his babysitter is. We actually kissed after class yesterday, though I pushed him off seconds before patrol almost caught us fraternizing. It's not like it's a criminal offense; I just didn't want Owen finding out.

"Isabella," Owen's voice calls from behind me. Speak of the devil.

I salute him, then curtsey. "Sergeant Bradshaw. What's up?"

"I'm going to need you to come with me."

A knot forms in my stomach and I don't know why. It's not like I have a reason to be nervous. "Did you get me a VIP fast pass or something?"

Owen smirks. "Something like that. Come on."

Owen leads me into the College of Social and Behavioral Sciences building, where the commanding Loyals reside. I'm reminded of the time when I was called into the principal's office for smoking weed in high school. I feel guilty, even though I haven't done anything wrong. Or have I? I knew that Austin's friends were trying to escape and I didn't say anything.

"Relax," Owen says. "You're not in trouble."

"It feels like I'm about to get detention … Just tell me what's going on, please. You're giving me anxiety."

He shakes his head. "It's more fun watching you squirm for a change."

We take the stairs up to the third floor and he knocks on an office door.

"It's open," a deep voice replies.

Owen turns the knob and gestures for me to enter first. Slouching behind the desk in an armchair is a black guy that's buff as all hell with a thick-ass beard. Near the window, there's a hot blonde girl with brown roots and big brown eyes sitting with her legs crossed. I've seen them both a few nights ago getting off of a helicopter that came in from the front lines. Owen tells me they were disgruntled soldiers from the Army before they joined Richard Thomas's movement, like most Loyals.

"Isabella, this is Lieutenant Freddy 'Dozer' Holt, San Bernardino base commander, and Sergeant Elsa 'Hellcat' Crawford, his second in command."

I extend a hand to Sergeant Crawford like this is a damn job interview. "Nice to finally meet you, Ms. Monroe," she says, examining me as we shake.

I raise an eyebrow. "Any particular reason Loyals as important as yourselves wanted to meet with little ol' me?"

"Bradshaw here's been talking you up, saying you've got the mindset of a Decider," Holt responds. "Figured he wanted you promoted to a position where he'd be allowed to fuck you."

"Charmed," I say.

Owen shakes his head and heads for the door.

Crawford opens a folder, spreading out the contents. The top two files are my police records with my horrible mugshots. Pretty sure there's a screenshot of my camgirl profile near the bottom. "A pretty thick FBI watchlist file for someone your age. You're even on the No Fly List."

"Exercise your First Amendment rights and that's what happens, I guess."

"Seems you were a big proponent of the Second Amendment," Holt says, setting down a screenshot of one of my Facebook rants.

"Well, I'm a Texan. We're firm believers that our guns are the only thing keeping tyranny at bay."

"Multiple arrests ..." Crawford adds.

"That's what happens when you protest in Freedom of Speech zones or record cops abusing peaceful protesters ..."

"You're on our list as well," Holt says. "A candidate for a special track of sorts."

"Wow!" I smile. "What an honor!"

Crawford nods. "Oh, it surely is. The list is quite short."

"May I ask what this special track entails?"

"That depends on you. Maybe recruitment? You were a psychology major, after all. And we've been watching you. You seem to be good with people. You also seem to have a knack for manipulating men, as noted by working Corporal Anderson and Sergeant Bradshaw. Yes, we've noticed ..." She smirks. "That could be a very useful talent."

"According to your social media accounts," Holt says, "you weren't afraid to record injustices from the front lines. And your father was a military man, so maybe there's fight in your blood. Maybe you enlist, bleed for the cause, and prove your worth. You've got the mind and potential to be in gray one day. Hell, you could be the next Anne Buckingham."

That's flattering. Commander Buckingham has become a bit of a role model of mine. A smart, beautiful, bad-ass woman unleashing hell on the creeps who've oppressed us for so long. Despite her fame and power, she still fights in the trenches alongside her comrades to reshape the world with bullets and fists.

If it isn't clear from the Fed's dossier on me, I'm a Decider by nature. There's no doubt that I want to be a part of their movement. The question is, to what capacity? After learning about Veritas, there's nothing I want to do more than fight against anyone working to back the world the Elites wanted to create. Do I want to get shot at? No. But no soldier does. Our enemy is powerful and numerous. Every boot on the ground is going to make the difference between winning and losing this war against corruption. And Holt was right. There's fight in me. I'm scrappy as hell, I can use a gun, I know some self-defense, and I've wanted to kick some ass since my dad died.

"Someone wanna point me in the direction of the barracks?" I ask.

Both Loyals grin.

Holt reaches under his desk and pulls out a uniform: black boots, a burgundy combat shirt, and fatigues similar to those worn by the Vanguards, but with the burgundy mixed in the gray and white pattern instead of black. "Welcome to the Deciders, soldier," he says.

5
METTLE

March 31

THE VANGUARDS ARE the lowest tier of the Deciders and many of them are mercenaries. The only thing keeping them from changing sides for a better offer are those blinking Marionette belts that the Loyals can detonate with wrist-mounted smart devices called Nevrons. Others are prisoners who, as Elsa has informed me, will be culled during "Act II's Purge" once their purpose has been served. But most Vanguards are soldiers who were duped into wearing Marionettes by Decider moles and by coerced commanding officers so that they could destroy militaries from within. If the threat of being blown up wasn't enough, their families were gathered up and held hostage in concentration camps where they were used as collateral. But that's all the higher-ups tell us. And that makes me wonder why Vanguards don't keep looking for a way to break free, save their loved ones, and try to rebel.

If I'm going to risk my life for the Deciders' cause, I want to know all of the variables and the dirty secrets that might screw me over one day. So I went looking for some. On the evening of my last night in San Bernardino, I hiked to the edge of camp where some Vanguards were often posted and looked for a mark to prod for information.

You can always tell the U.S. soldiers who are forced to fight from the mercenaries. It's all in the eyes, and the U.S. soldiers' burn red-hot like they're about to go postal. I found a chisel-faced hunk, one Corporal Sanders according to his uniform. I ran my hand across the fence while I made some small talk. When it seemed like he was comfortable with me, I played at being a scared girl who was questioning what she was getting into. Sanders told me that the Vanguards who attempted to rebel early in the Annex had to watch their relatives be executed on a live stream before they were killed as well.

Killing innocents? That doesn't sit well with me at all. But I guess those murders were no different than the Psycho Nerve Agent attacks and war they waged on cities that I convinced myself was an acceptable atrocity in the name of saving humanity. And to the best of my knowledge, no more civilians have actually been killed since. So long as it stays that way, I guess I'll keep fighting the good fight.

Vanguards who can demonstrate that they're truly loyal to the Deciders will join those of us from the reeducation camps who have been sent up here to northern Washington for training. Together, we will form a new tier of Deciders known as the Enforcers, the main fighting force that will keep the reactionaries in check.

Nine days in, things aren't terrible yet. Years of dancing and 5K fun runs have my cardio in stellar condition. As for hand-to-hand combat, I'm eh. My dad taught me enough to fend off men who were too big to overpower—throat strikes, eye pokes, groin kicks—and I've taken some kickboxing classes, but I still have a hell of a long way to go.

My bare-knuckle sparring session today was against Slim Tim. The poor guy tried to take it easy on me and I punched him square in the mouth, then put him in a chokehold. My knuckles are missing some skin after meeting his teeth so I bandage myself up real quick before I hike on over to the range. It's a bit warm out so I pin up my hair and shed my camo jacket.

Sergeant Crawford oversees our weapons training on the days she's not handling warfighting duties with Holt in their new theater of Seattle. Once our group is done with the rifle and pistol range, she takes us to the run-and-gun course. It's a mile's worth of targets, obstacles, and props that we have to navigate around and shoot through to hit targets of different sizes and distances. I nail a good number of targets, except for a few distance shots. The groupings are getting tighter and my weapon swap time and reload speed are far smoother and quicker than in previous days.

When I reach the final part of the course, I shoot through the window, run out the doorway, and crouch behind the car. I fire off two shots over the hood at one target, go prone and hit another, then dash toward the sandbags, draw my pistol, and hit the last target poking out from behind a wall.

Crawford stops the timer. "Not bad," she says. "You're definitely improving, but your aim is still lacking compared to the rest of your training group."

Panting, I nod and holster my pistol. "I'll get there eventually."

"You better get there soon. Never know when we'll need you on the frontlines, Monroe."

I was last up on the course today, so everyone else is gone when we get back to the Humvee. Crawford and I shoot the shit while she drives us back to camp. Maybe because we have a similar sense of humor, I get a strong older-sister vibe from her, which is nice because I've always had to look out for myself on top of caring for my younger sister.

During the ride, we go from talking about drunken hookup stories to me somehow bringing up Zach Schmidt. He was my most recent ex-boyfriend, the sweetest guy I've ever met, my first love, the guy I probably would've spent the rest of my life with if I didn't royally screw things up … Ugh … When he found out what I'd been doing behind his back, that nice guy I fell for turned into a savage asshole in the blink of an eye. Zach slut-shamed me all over social media, telling everyone in essay-length posts what I'd done. He leaked all my nudes to his buddies and revenge porn sites. He outed me as a stripper to my friends and family. The fallout was so bad, but I guess I deserved it …

I segue into talking about guys we're interested in on base. When she asks what was going on between Owen and me, I have to confess.

"I fucking knew you two would get it on!" she says. "When did it happen?"

"The night before we left, he invited me to his room for dinner and wine. I figured he deserved a parting gift."

"And how was the Sergeant Bradshaw experience?"

I scrunch up my face. "Eh, mediocre at best. He barely got the condom on before he finished."

Elsa cackles. "Want me to get him transferred up here for you, or are you moving on to Dunn?"

"Ew, no! He's like a brother to me. You know that …"

"Just teasing you. What about, Uber Austin? I see how you look at him. Afraid of breaking his heart?"

"Something like that. He'd probably propose as soon as I showed him a bra strap."

At the split before the barracks, Crawford hangs a right instead of a left.

"I think you missed your turn, Sarge."

"Oh, didn't anyone tell you?" she asks with a menacing grin. "Phase Two of training starts today ..."

She pulls up outside a utility building a quarter-mile from camp. There's a transport truck and two Loyals standing outside of the door. Crawford leads me inside, taking me through a series of hallways before we come to a rusty door.

"What're we doing here?" I ask.

She hands me a magazine for my SIG Sauer and a combat knife. "One of the hardest things for any sane, empathetic person to do is to kill another human being in cold blood. On the battlefield, that first time you put another person in your sights, hesitation strikes. I can attest to that because it happened to me in Iraq. So today's lesson is about stamping out that hesitation from your mind through exposure therapy."

"You're going to have me kill someone? Who?" I ask, trying to sound like I'm not panicking.

"We've been bringing enemy combatants back here for interrogations and ... training purposes. I'm going to send you into that room and, when I give the signal, a guard on the other side will release one of the POWs. Maybe they'll have a gun. Maybe they'll have a knife. Either way, if you don't put them down, they'll try to end you. Understand?"

I nod.

"You said you might have killed a Psycho-maddened man during the Annex, right? So this should be a bit easier for you than it was for the others."

I open the door and step into a boiler room. There are some rusty patches on the tile floor, probably dried blood from the earlier executions. The only sound comes from water dripping somewhere in the room.

I stand there, slightly hunched forward, gripping my pistol with both hands. Time passes and the door at the other end of the room still doesn't open. Fear creeps into my mind and I start wondering if the target is already in here with me, hiding, waiting for me to start hunting for them. Then the door creaks open and a man in tattered Army fatigues stumbles inside as though he was pushed. He's dirty as hell and his lip is split. His eyes are wild with a mix of anger and fear. There's something in his hand, but it's too dark in here to make out what it is.

He looks at the pistol then up at me. "You don't have to do this," he says, stepping forward slowly. "I just want to get out of here so I can find my family." He takes a second step, then a third and a fourth. "I'm not the enemy."

I don't say anything. I just raise my pistol. When I do, he charges. And the gap closes fast. When he's almost on top of me, his knife glints in the light from above.

I fire, twice. He drops, groaning and squirming. He tries crawling away, and I put a round into his head to end his suffering.

The door opens again. It's another soldier, taller and more bruised than the last. He notices the body and immediately darts to his left. I catch him in midstride. Two more soldiers enter the room soon after, a guy and a girl this time. Panic sets in and I start firing wildly at both of them, unsure of which target to down fist. I get the guy, but the girl escapes to cover.

Breathing more heavily than I'd like to, I pursue her. Her shadowy form flits between pair of boilers and I fire. The gun locks open afterward—I'm out of ammo.

I holster the pistol and draw the combat knife. As I near the transformers, she bursts out and pounces. Instinctively, I bring the knife up and plunge it into her chest as she tackles me to the floor.

The knife jumps with each heartbeat like the blade is right up against her atrium …

She claws at my face. "Traitor …" she spits.

I grab a fistful of her hair and pull until she rolls a bit to the side. Then, I withdraw the knife and stab her again and again until she collapses back on top of me. Warmth spreads across my combat shirt and my hands get slick. I can smell it, that metallic tinge of blood. When I finally snap out of the shock, I grab her by the jacket and shove her off of me. I can barely keep my grip on the knife as I scramble to my feet, trying to stand on wobbly legs.

As I bend over to puke, the door squeals again. I raise my knife only to lower it a second later when Sergeant Crawford emerges from the shadows.

She claps her hands. "Well done."

I scan the bodies. "You said there would only be one."

"Sometimes you get intel and it's wrong. Lesson learned."

I puke again.

Crawford pats my back. "It only gets easier from here, babe."

April 29

I'm trembling, not from how cold it is in here, but from fear of what's about to happen. I was on my way to go tinkle in a porta potty a few nights ago when someone slipped a bag over my head, roughed me up, then dragged me into a truck. Now I'm in the basement of some building and being interrogated by guys in U.S. Army fatigues. They ask me about our base and operation. Of course I don't say shit because I figure this is another part of my training. Even if it isn't, it's not like I know enough to satisfy them anyway.

They start with waterboarding. When that doesn't work, they get to shocking me with a cattle prod. Then I get slapped around and beaten with a baton. Maybe an hour passes before they decide to take a break and leave me in the room with some Swedish death metal blaring through the speakers. I'm bleary as hell but after ten minutes or an hour or two, I realize it's the same song playing in a loop.

Eventually, they come back and it starts over again. Except, this time, they don't bother to ask me anything. When they're done, they chain my arms to an overhead pipe with just enough slack for me to balance my feet on a wobbling ammo can. I slip soon after and shriek in pain as I slowly spin back and forth like the world's most traumatized tetherball.

I guess they think I've broken because they free my wrists and take me to another room. I'm chained to a bloodstained wooden table across from a man in dressed in fatigues with a black ski mask over his face. There's a sharp-ass knife in his hand so I can't imagine anything good is going to follow.

"Tell me the location of the Decider bases in Seattle!" he demands, placing his knife against the back of my hand.

"I told you I don't know shit!" I cry, spitting everywhere. "Just let me go! Or just kill me, bitch!"

With a quick pass of the knife, he slices the back of my hand and I scream so loud that it burns my throat.

The questions keep coming and so do the cuts. The bastard's making inch-long incisions on my hands, fingers, and arms until I'm an unresponsive, trembling, sniveling mess. He wipes off the knife and pulls out a nail gun, then pins down my left hand. "Last chance," he snarls.

My mouth is bone dry but I manage to work up enough saliva to spit in his face.

There's a puff and then searing pain. I try to yank my hand away, but it's nailed to the table. I shriek like my mind's being ripped to pieces.

"That's enough!" a man demands from behind me. "She passed. Get her to recovery!"

That was a test? Are you fucking kidding me?

The man in the ski mask sticks a syringe in my hand near the nail and presses down the plunger. It must have been a painkiller because it doesn't hurt when he pulls out the nail. "Sorry I had to do that to you," he whispers, unshackling my wrist. "We all have to go through it …"

I wake up in a hospital room. There's an IV in my inner elbow and bandages on my arms and hands. My wounds all have this weird tingly feeling. I poke one to see how much it hurts, an attempt to gauge how much time has passed. There's some dull pain, but not much.

"Feeling better than you'd thought, huh?" says the man in the bed next to me. "That's the Cascade working."

I sit up, looking over at him. It's Benny from my training group.

"It speeds up healing and reduces the pain to almost nothing," he adds. "Apparently it's some next-gen shit that was being kept from the public. Nurse said they put something in the IV too."

"Well, what a bunch of sweethearts," I mutter.

"They're just trying to make us strong, Monroe."

"Yeah, yeah," I groan, lying back down and turning my attention back to the TV on the wall across from us. Decider Global News is on and a message from Richard Thomas is about to air.

While I wait for it to start, I think back to a month ago when Crawford said that it would get easier from here. The day after I murdered those soldiers, word came down from the Architect that the next phase, Purge, had begun and we trainees had to exterminate the convicts who'd been pulled out of prison and made into Vanguards. So we lined them up in front of a trench and lit them up. It's not hard to do when you can tell yourself you're aiming at a pedophile or a murderer. Even the cleanup wasn't so bad—they brought in a couple of backhoes to shovel dirt over the corpses.

My fear of killing had been extinguished. My aim is somewhat on point. I could probably take down most guys twice my size in a hand-to-hand street fight even if they had some training. Things were getting easier and I was proud to be joining an army that's changing the world. And after this "torture resilience" bullshit, well, shit, the only thing I'm sure of is that I hate that little bitch Elsa for betraying my trust.

"The terrorists calling themselves the Angels of War Militia," Richard Thomas says, "attacked several small towns and Decider bases, killing not only my men, but civilians as well." There's a montage of civilian corpses arranged around winged circle-A's. Security footage shows the guerilla fighters engaging our people. They're dressed in all-black civilian clothes and some of them are wearing our Deva helmets.

"To the Angels of War, know this," Richard continues. "Your crimes will not go unpunished. In due time, you *will be caught.* And when you are, you *will* be dealt the most severe punishment."

"We should nuke those bastards," Benny says. "Them and anybody who doesn't turn them in."

"Sure, sure," I scoff. "Or maybe we should just carpet bomb them with Veritas books so they understand why they're wrong. Then they'll be throwing themselves at us to join the cause."

6
FRACTURING

May 24

AUSTIN AND I creep through the woods, leading with our rifles as we scan for threats. Our camouflage is a forest green and gray variant of the gear we typically train in, so as long as we take it slow, we won't stand out too much. Between the crunching leaves and snapping branches, the loudest sound out here is my growling stomach. Or maybe it's Austin's.

Today marks the second-to-last day of our escape and evasion training. We had to escape "capture" then flee into the woods, acquiring weapons, gear, and sustenance along the way. If we were recaptured, more torture awaited us. Though my body healed up weeks ago, my mind hasn't, and I couldn't suffer through that again. On the plus side, they might kill me before I'm caught … Though our weapons are loaded with nonlethal wax bullets, Crawford warned us that some of the Hunters might be using live rounds.

Austin, a younger kid named Will, and I were the only members of our E&E group to successfully escape the Hunters. We evaded their patrols and eventually linked up with another team of four trainees from a different group, two of whom are from Camp San Bernardino—Slim Tim and Jason Dunn, or Kappa, as we call him. For the past six days, we've been bouncing between different campsites, fending off the enemy during scavenging runs or when they tried storming our camps. Austin, Will, Kappa, a guy whose name I can never remember, and I are all that's left of our band.

Water hasn't been an issue. There are a few freshwater sources nearby, enough to hit at random and avoid Hunter patrols. Our food, however, ran out yesterday morning, so Austin and I have ventured out to find some more while the others defend our camp.

I stumble across some wild mint that I gather for some tea later. At one of the snares we set two days ago, we find a rabbit. Between scanning for threats, I steal some looks at Austin while he guts and skins the carcass. Like the rest of the men who enlisted, his once-shaggy hair has been buzzed down. It's grown back a bit, but I miss the way it was—that old look suited him. The beard he's been growing out is kind of working for me though. Those kind, greenish blue eyes of his seem steely now, encompassed by dark rings from lack of sleep. In the few hours he does manage to get rest, he thrashes as his subconscious struggles to make sense of the lives he was forced to take and the torture he's endured. I don't sleep too well either.

I nudge him to get his attention, but he doesn't even glance in my direction. "Can we focus on the mission please?" is all he says.

I can feel our friendship fracturing, and I think I'm one wrong step from making it shatter ... because I'm good at ruining things.

Though he won't say it, I can tell he resents me. He's here because of me, after all. I talked him out of escaping the reeducation camp, and though I never asked him to, he followed me up here because I enlisted without ever making it clear where we stood after that one kiss. I manipulated him to keep him wanting me, to keep him around. It's a pattern of mine—an addiction to the thrill of being lusted after paired with the fear of being abandoned. It's cowardly and selfish, and a habit I just can't seem to break. And I'm not sure if it's because Austin's life is on the line because of me, but what I've done to him is making me feel even guiltier than I did after what I'd done to Zach …

A helicopter beats against the air overhead and we hunker down in a shelter that our team crafted out of some leaves, netting, and camouflaged tarp. I set our metal cup over the small fire to heat up some water for mint tea. "Looks like we get to enjoy this whole rabbit by ourselves!" I say, nudging him.

Austin saws off a leg from the rabbit and skewers it with a sharpened branch. "Lucky us, a five-star meal …"

I scowl. None of us are who we were when the Deciders brought us in. My old Camp San Bernardino crew was full of a bunch of goofballs. Now everyone's a hell of a lot more serious and all about eradicating anyone who doesn't agree with the Decider way. I can't really tell how much I've changed. I'm definitely less trusting and more radical in my beliefs. There's no doubt that I'm a bit colder. I feel myself becoming less sassy and more hostile as the days go by. Still, I value human life. Everyone else seems gung-ho to spill the blood of anyone who doesn't agree with us. And me? Well, I just want to change the minds of the ignorant.

During whatever downtime I get between training, I've been keeping up with the reports from the fights against the Angels of War. New intel suggests that their militia is being led by some college boy with support from a band of former Marines. Recently, the militia's numbers have boomed from a few hundred to nearly a thousand soldiers after teaming up with a National Guard contingent and Maryland-based rebels called the Frederick Militia. Since then, it seems they've become a real problem for our main force. The last report I've read before E&E training began said that they managed to capture General Hawthorne but we got them back by sacking their base in Quantico. Who knows how many of them got out. Most of them, I hope. My friends might be lusting for their annihilation, but I just want these rebels to understand how wrongheaded their resistance really is.

Stomachs full of grilled rabbit, Austin and I sit shoulder to shoulder under our shelter, watching the rain as we sip the mint and pine needle tea that I concocted for a soothing boost of Vitamin C.

"This doesn't taste terrible," Austin says after an obnoxious slurp.

"Drink any louder and they'll hear us back at camp …"

"Ha. Ha."

"Do you hate me?" I ask.

"Where the hell did that come from?"

"I can't help but feel that all the shit you've gone through since we met is because of me. You know, because …" I let my words trail off. "Never mind."

"Because what?"

"Because you're in love with me or some shit …"

"And who said I was in love with you?"

"You enlisted in a war to fight for ideals you don't believe in because you wanted to be by my side. What would you call that if not love?"

He pokes at the fire with his stick. "Madness."

I snort. "Yeah, maybe that's a better word, hon."

He just stares at me, disgusted. "Knock it off with that 'hon' bullshit. Stop fucking teasing me if you don't feel the same way as I do. It's fucked up."

"I'm sorry, I can't help being … this way."

"You can't help jerking people around in order to get what you want?"

"That's not what this is! I care about you. A lot!"

"Just like you cared about that Loyal you screwed to get out of yard duty?"

"Yeah, I flirted with him to get what I wanted. But I didn't sleep with him until I caught feelings. I ain't that kind of girl."

"And you fell for a … *terrorist*. You chose that instead of me?"

"Hypocritical much? He's fighting for the same cause that I am. That hasn't stopped you from deciding that I'm your fucking soul mate or whatever."

Austin tosses the dregs of the fire and starts to stand up but I grab his arm.

"And I never said I didn't have feelings for you, Austin. You've just been assuming. Maybe I don't think I'm good enough for you."

Austin shakes his head. "Oh please …"

"Maybe I don't know what I want. Maybe I'm avoiding romance so I can focus on fighting for what I believe in. Maybe I'm worried that we'll end up on opposite sides of this war."

"People have split up for less, I guess," he grumbles.

I set my tea down and lean my head against his shoulder. Eventually, he rests his head on mine and takes my hand. We sit there like that for a while, playing with each other's fingers. After some time, I sit up, brush my curls out of my face, and stare at him. Slowly, I bring my face closer to his. "Take me now or you won't get another chance," I whisper.

The poor guy looks confused. His eyes search mine. Then he pulls me in. We make out for a minute then I force him onto his back and get to work unbuckling his pants.

Austin sleeps beside me while I sit and scan the woods. And by watching the woods, I mean daydreaming, replaying what happened between us an hour ago. It was passionate and it was rough in the right way. Almost three months' worth of near-death experiences and pent-up sexual tension and frustration will do that, I suppose. But beneath the passion, guilt bubbles. What happened was a one-time deal. I plan on letting him know that once this training is over. And if he can't accept it? Well, maybe I can get Crawford to transfer him out east so he can defect to the Angels of War. I smirk at the thought.

Brush rustles ahead. Something splashes in a puddle behind us. I ball-tap Austin and he springs up.

"What the shit, Izzy?" he groans.

"Contacts," I whisper. "We're surrounded."

"Shit," he says, grabbing his rifle and following me out.

"Stand down!" a man shouts.

I burst out of cover and fire at the Loyal who steps out of the brush. Austin does the same to whoever's on the right. The men flinch and cuss. No one returns fire. An air horn blows.

"Austin! Izzy! Chill!" Kappa shouts, waving his arms. "Hold your damn fire!"

"Goddammit, that shit hurt!" the Loyal I shot shouts. As my bloodlust dims, I recognize him as Staff Sergeant Cody Dietrich. "Shit's ending a day early. Don't worry, everyone passed. We need you back at base pronto!"

"What happened?" I yell.

"The Angels of War are attacking DC," Dietrich says. "And things aren't looking good for us ..."

7
THE FALL

May 29

BETWEEN THE TIME we left the training grounds and returned to camp, those goddamn Angels of War somehow freed the Vanguards in DC. Twenty-five-hundred grunts banded with the militia and fucking decimated our forces and the Vanguards who remained loyal them. Richard Thomas was forced to order an evac and level the entire city with an antimatter warhead—some real science fiction shit that I can't even comprehend. But that didn't stop them. Worse, the Architect's helicopter got shot down somewhere on the other side of the Chesapeake and we haven't heard from him in the five days since. Anne Buckingham and the other founding members of the Deciders have gone missing too. Not good.

Things have been in disarray since. All bases are on constant high alert. And after nine long weeks, training has come to an end and my group was inducted into the Decider army as privates. Rumors that we might be shipping out east have been circulating since.

It's fifteen after midnight. I'm sitting in Elsa's office, feet on the coffee table and a beer in my hand, reading through some intel on a tablet while she's coordinating with Holt and other higher-ups over sat phone. She snaps her fingers and mouths the word *message*.

"Hold on, I'm about to listen to it right now." She sets the phone down.

I open the message that just popped up and play the attached audio recording. It's a distress call from Anne Buckingham to Norfolk Command sent a few minutes ago.

"The Angels of War captured me during the fight in DC," Anne says in her aristocratic accent. "Richard was brought in hours later after being shot down in Maryland. We tried to escape … I got away. He didn't. The Angels of War still have him!"

"My queen, where is he being held?" Loyal Lieutenant Ralph Perry, Eastern Command Norfolk, asks.

"They were holding us in Culpeper. There's no telling how long they will keep him alive so I want you to send everyone you have in Norfolk there now! And I mean *everyone*!"

Elsa shakes her head. "Ooh, I wish I was in Virginia! I want to be there for the slaughter."

"Don't we have a supersonic jet somewhere?" I ask. "We could be there in an hour."

"Yeah, I'm pretty sure Echelon has the jet checked out," she grumbles.

I raise an eyebrow.

Sirens wail, startling me out of my sleep. *A tornado*, I think, but then I remember that I'm not in Texas anymore.

I spring up from Elsa's office couch and grab the tablet. It's 3:41 A.M. and there's a message on the screen. It reads:

DEAR DECIDERS,

THE WORLD IS NOT YOURS.

SINCERELY,

THE ANGELS OF WAR

┍∩┑ (☝_◢) ┍∩┑

"What the shit is this?" I close it so I can see the message hidden beneath the pop-up. It's a red alert to all Decider forces.

The door bursts open and light floods in. Through squinting eyes, all I see is Elsa's silhouette holding a rifle. Another rifle is slung over her back. "Gear up, Private! All warfighters in the area are needed in Seattle."

"Wait, what's going on?" I groan. Elsa shoves the rifle into my hands. "Norfolk was just hit," she says, "and I don't know how but whatever those bastards did to free the Vanguards in DC has been replicated everywhere."

"Wait, what?"

We burst outside and double-time it to Dozer's trailer. "You heard me right! Our whole army just got caught with their pants down. We need to get control of strong points before those revenge-bent puppets overthrow us."

My eyes are wide and I can't get them to blink. *It's real*, I think. It's really happening. I'm going to get shot at, maybe killed.

Elsa throws open the door to Dozer's trailer. He holds up a hand, telling us to wait.

"Word came in from a DC survivor that Richard Thomas was killed by the Dark Angel five days ago," a man growls over the radio. "That story about him being captured was a diversion."

My eyes burn as tears start to well up. Richard Thomas, my idol, my hero, killed by the AOW leader, Dion Johnson. Elsa showed me the dossier on the college senior a few days ago when it was released. I remember thinking he wasn't bad looking for a bad guy. And that says something because I don't usually go for black dudes. Intelligence gathered from Angels of War POWs confirmed that he went from being a party boy with zero military training to militia grunt to leader in the time it took me to complete training. That shouldn't impress me, but it does. Actually, for him to be skilled and charismatic enough to become their leader while also being so misguided and close minded to the truth, it makes me worry what kind of monster we have on our hands. What concerns me the most is the fact that after only being a "soldier" for a few months, his file says that he personally tortures the Deciders his people capture.

"Not only did we lose our leader," another guy responds, "but sixty percent of our army has turned against us … Shit!"

"Echelon will deal with this," the first voice replies. "Stand by for orders."

What in the hell is Echelon?

"I'm ready to spill some blood," Elsa growls. "How about you?"

Holt grabs up the LMG from against the wall. "Anyone not with us is catching a bullet this morning!" He chambers a round.

The trucks drop us off at the airfield. Loyals hand us weapons from containers of equipment. We're also given Nevrons— basically a wrist-mounted smartphone that the Loyals used to communicate. This was also the device used to detonate the Marionettes of Vanguards who got out of line.

Just like the day we were herded into Cal State San Bernardino, Austin is right in front of me. This time, he hasn't looked back at me once.

The day after we had sex, we ran into each other after breakfast and he pulled me aside to talk. We took a walk in the woods and he backed me into a tree and started kissing me. I let it go on for longer than I should have before I pushed him off.

"What's wrong?" Austin asked.

"Yesterday … We're not a thing now …"

He scowled.

"I just wanted to give you the … thank you that you wanted."

"Fucking hell!" he shouted. "I don't want a thank you! I don't want sex! I want you, Isabella!"

"I'm sorry, Austin, but me and you? That's never going to happen."

That was the last time we spoke. Now we're about to go into combat and this resentful sap is on my squad, thanks to Elsa thinking he's still playing bodyguard. I'm hoping my other squad mates will watch my back out there. And Elsa will cap him if he does something stupid to endanger me …

June 18

The restaurant is dead ahead. Bullets rip through the air as I follow Slim Tim and Austin across the street. I slip behind a white pickup and sight the enemy through my scope. On the other side of the crosshairs among the National Guardsmen are soldiers wearing black combat tops and Vanguard camouflaged pants. But they aren't Vanguards anymore. The resistance calls them Insurgents and they identify as Angels of War so much that they even tag their territories with that same stupid winged circle-A.

The enemy scatters like roaches from my suppressive fire. Then they start shooting back. The moment I see an opening, I book it. A rocket crashes out of a third-floor window and hits the Humvee and the Insurgents who are covering behind it with a thunderous boom. At the same time, Slim Tim hits the ground.

"*Arggh! Shit!*" he howls, holding his leg.

The Loyals and Enforcers in the building cover us from the windows while we pick him up and help him to safety.

Today's no worse than the last fifteen days. If anything, we're taking fewer losses. It's hard to tell since our satellites are down. Whatever the Angels of War did when they emancipated the

Vanguards also crippled our network, forcing us to rely on rudimentary shortwave radios, and even those are being jammed.

The first few days were a shock. Being shot at with live rounds, seeing friends and comrades getting their heads blown off, having their blood smeared across your visor ... it really fucks you up. On the first day, I collapsed in fear behind an armored truck. Kappa and Austin had to run out into enemy fire and drag me back behind the defensive line. Hellcat pounced on me and pressed a gun against my forehead, threatening to shoot me if I didn't do what I was trained to do. Since then I've fought, though there were a few times after that where I just spaced out and started wandering around like a sleepwalker. Thankfully Austin was there to tackle me out of the line of fire each time.

"We're losing this city," Dozer says. "Just like Virginia and Texas. Fuck! I'm calling it. Clear us a path out of here. We'll fight to the river then hold our ground until we get the signal."

"You three," Crawford says to Austin, Patrick, and me, "flank around and pick off that last fire team."

I nod and lead the way. Head on a swivel, I scan all windows, doorways, and alleys for potential threats. When a soldier in a black shirt and Army camo pants pops out around the corner, I yell "Contact" as I dart into a doorway while spraying rounds at him like a novice would. I guess it doesn't matter because he goes down anyway.

At the next corner, three shots ring off and I react instinctively—skidding to a stop, taking a knee, and punching out the rifle at the threat. Patrick is eating asphalt, blood pooling around him. For some reason, Austin is aiming at him. It takes a few seconds for it to click that he's the one who shot our squadmate in the back ... And when Patrick twitches and gasps for air, Austin puts one last round in the base of his skull.

"Austin, what the fuck are you doing?" I ask.

Austin tosses his helmet and his Nevron. His face is sweaty, and his eyes are wide and unblinking. "I'm leaving! I won't betray my country any longer! Don't you fucking try and stop me!" He jabs his gun toward me.

"Chill." I lower my rifle, letting it hang. "Do what you want, buddy."

He walks backward, his wild eyes scanning the buildings looking down at us. "Come with me. Make the right decision, Isabella."

I shake my head.

"The Angels of War have won. It's over. Don't piss away your life like this. Fuck, even the Germans surrendered after Hitler died."

"Go ahead," I say. "I'm willing to die for what I believe in."

"I won't let you." He raises his rifle and pulls the trigger.

PART TWO

FOR THE CAUSE

8
ICEWORM

June 18

I FALL BACK onto my ass, eyes blurry from tears, breathing through gritted teeth as I fight the urge to unleash a shriek that will surely summon the enemy.

There's so much blood. I'm lightheaded and panicking, frantically trying to stop the hemorrhaging while also trying to work my radio at the same time. "Hellcat?" I gasp into the mic, my voice trembling. "Do you copy? Patrick was KIA and I'm hit! Austin ... Austin's chasing the shooter." I don't know why I didn't rat that bastard out.

"Sit tight!" Crawford responds. "We just handled our targets and we're on the way!"

They turn the corner just as I tighten the tourniquet around my leg. Elsa patches me up with some Cascade and bandages. When I'm good to go, Dunn slings my arm over his shoulders and leads me over to where Slim Tim is sitting in the back of a Knight XV armored truck, his bandaged leg extended straight out in front of him. Three of the Enforcers staving off the threat are gunned down before I dive into the back beside him. My eyes linger on the dead we've left behind and I start wondering if I'd be lying there beside them had Austin not incapacitated me.

Judging from the chatter on my radio, we're getting absolutely wrecked, and it sounds like there's another wave coming our way. The second my team clears the immediate threats, Dozer, Crawford, Dunn, and a few stragglers who were separated from their units pile in and we drive back to the bay. While everyone else works to hold off the enemy, Tim and I, along with other injured soldiers, are taken to the triage station that's been set up in the Maritime Building, a white office building not far from what looks like a pier. Explosions coming from multiple directions shake the ground beneath my cot.

"What's happening?" I ask.

The soldier next to me shrugs. "All I know is that those are our bombs."

The explosions continue for another half an hour, which is oddly a comfort because it's been drowning out the groans of the guy next to me. His left leg and arm are just bloody stumps, and seeing the condition he's in makes me worry that they might amputate my leg even though the medic assured me no arteries or bones were hit. Acrid air starts seeping into the triage room so those of us not hooked up to ventilators have to put on our Deva helmets to avoid coughing up a lung. From my cot, I have a clear view of the entrance and the window beside it. As buildings collapse and the friendly shelling approaches our location, the visibility outside worsens by the minute. Several silhouettes appear behind the haze, charging toward the entrance. Elsa, Dozer, and their team charge inside, soot coming down like flurries behind them.

"It's go time!" Dozer commands, waving for us to file out. "Move! Move! Move!"

A dark gray layer of ash powders me as Elsa helps me stagger across the street toward Coleman Dock. I stare in awe at the line of warships raining hell on the city behind us. Dozens of helicopters are idling in the Seattle Ferry parking lot. Most of our people are boarding the naval ships docked at the ferry pier. Others are jumping in small boats and racing off to naval ships that are barely visible in the middle of the bay. As we approach a white Chinook, jets roar overhead, adding their contributions to the inferno below.

"Where the hell are we going now?" I shout. "Vancouver?"

Elsa gives me that Cheshire grin of hers. "Think bigger! And colder!"

July 4

If anyone's feeling guilty for losing Seattle, they shouldn't bother. Seems we got our asses kicked all over the world. Two days ago, we got word from whoever's in charge that it was time to go underground. I don't know where the others are hiding, but we've been sent to the wilderness of Alaska and Canada—nothing but moose, lichen, and oil pipelines. I asked Elsa who sent us to this frozen hell and she said Echelon. And when I asked what the hell Echelon was, she told me to "*shut the fuck up.*"

We actually started in Anchorage but retreated east when a band of Russian and American forces arrived. A large group of us fled to Fort Yukon. Two weeks later the select few of us chosen for extraction were loaded into a plane with a wingspan that's twice the length of a basketball court and cast out into the frigid air.

During our descent, this son of a bitch starts vibrating like crazy. My eyes are shut so hard they ache and I'm hyperventilating to the point that I might black out.

The landing is a bit rough, but we're not cooking alive in a raging fireball on the runway so no complaints there. When the cargo door drops, wind gusts in and strips the heat from my bones.

The air only gets colder as I limp down the ramp. I step off to the side for a moment, set down my duffle bag, and take in everything from the icebergs floating in the water to the mountains in the north. All I know about this place is that it's on Disko Island, Greenland, north of a town that begins with the letter Q whose name I can't pronounce.

"Stop acting like a basic bitch who's never been to Greenland before!" Elsa teases from up ahead, waving me forward.

I pick up my bag. "Stop acting like you have! What are we even doing here? This place makes Fort Yukon seem like fucking Malibu."

"They say the new regime set up here," Dozer says. "Got an underground bunker or some shit."

"Oh? And of everyone who made it out, they picked us?"

A smug smile stretches across his face. "I got connections."

A white truck pulls onto the airstrip, followed by white and gray troop carriers. From the lead truck, a tall redhead dressed in all white hops out of the passenger seat. "Welcome to Godhaven!" he announces. His voice sounds familiar for some reason. "The name is General Paul O'Brian. Load up your shit and we'll get you situated once we get to Iceworm."

I lean in toward Dozer. "Um, what the hell is an Iceworm?" He shrugs.

It takes less than an hour to load up our gear. Then we're off. Through the back of the truck, I see the cold waters recede as we ride down a road that has us all rocking like bobbleheads. Eventually, the night sky gives way to a tunnel made of jagged rock. As we descend down a ramp, a large door drops behind us, separating us from the outside world.

"Did we just drive into a mountain?" Tim asks.

The truck halts a minute later. Belongings in hand, I follow the others out into a cavernous vehicle bay where Loyals and a few men dressed in all white are waiting for us.

"Project Iceworm," O'Brian begins, his voice booming from a speaker system somewhere in the dark upper reaches of the cavern, "was a top-secret United States Cold War program to build bases and nuclear missile silos under the ice sheets. When that proved impractical, the project was moved further south from camps Fistclench and Century to the coasts. Its construction was done under the guise of a scientific research project investigating the composition of rock beneath the surface. When the Danish government came snooping, the project was scrapped and left incomplete. That is, until globalist elites revitalized the project and bribed the locals to keep them silent."

The general and his pack of Loyals and White Coats lead us through a blast door into a smaller tunnel. As he continues his orientation speech, I remember where I know his voice from. He was the one who announced over the radio that Richard Thomas had been killed on the day the Vanguards were turned.

"The command center, cafeteria, training facility, lab, R&D sector, hospital, and barracks are interconnected by a series of tunnels. The main base spans three kilometers and can comfortably accommodate five hundred personnel. This will be your home until it is time to reclaim what is ours. Everything above ground belongs to us as well, so if you're feeling claustrophobic feel free to put on your civilian camouflage and pretend to be an Eskimo with the locals. I wouldn't recommend that come winter ..."

At the end of the spiel, we come to an atrium of sorts. My squad and I get in one of the lines leading to the circular desk in the middle.

"There's a face I'd thought I'd never see again!" a familiar voice shouts.

"Owen!" I drop my duffle and greet him with a hug. "What are you doing here?"

"I kicked a whole lot of ass down in Texas and I guess my reward is to be at the forefront of whatever comes next. Got promoted to staff sergeant too."

I give him a salute. "Congratulations, sir."

"Oh, fuck off." He smiles. "It's good to see you. I heard Dozer's unit was coming in so I came down here to see if I could find you."

"Well, ain't you sweet, hon. Where's Shon?"

Owen shakes his head.

"Shit ... I'm sorry."

"Well, that's war, right?" He looks around. "And your chauffer-bodyguard-stalker friend?"

"Not sure ... We ... got split up during the retreat from Seattle."

"Damn, I'm sorry."

"Eh, maybe he's fine," I say. "He probably got out on his own or was picked up by another squad. I'd like to believe so, anyway."

"I'm sure he's alright." He touches my forearm and I pull away.

"Owen, if you have feelings for me I think it's better if you kept your distance. Feelings make shit complicated. And there's no place for that drama in an army, you know?"

Owen smiles. "Don't flatter yourself, sweetheart. I'll settle for being friends. Unless friends with benefits is an option ..."

I smile back. "Maybe we'll stick with just friends for now."

He looks down at his Nevron and taps the screen a few times. "Okay, we're synched up. I'll see you later maybe?"

"You bet."

I watch him until he disappears into the crowd, thinking back to that night and imagining a second round in some cozy cottage above ground. *Goddammit.*

Elsa nudges my arm. "Hey, looks like you found yourself—"

"Not now," I interrupt. "I'm not in the mood."

She smirks. "Yeah, but you will be."

"Can we not? Please?"

"Did I miss something? What the hell happened between you and Uber Austin that turned you into a nun?"

"I wouldn't tell you if you tortured me."

July 11

After finishing up cardio training at the gym, I decide to try be early to the meeting I was invited to by Dozer on behalf of General O'Brian. I've got a few extra minutes to kill so I end up taking the long way around to explore more of Iceworm while I listen to the latest briefing using the wireless headphones Owen gave me. The newly appointed President Ron Pell has merged the National Guard, the Air National Guard, Homeland Security, and the Coast Guard with the militia that caused us so much trouble to form a new military branch called the United States Angels of War, USAW for short. It's hard for me to fathom how, in a world post-Veritas, people can still idolize a militia that supports the old corrupt way of government and elitism. I probably should've kept listening to my workout playlist because now I'm just irritated …

The tunnel I find myself in is smaller than the others and desolate as hell. Eventually it spits me out by the genetics laboratory. There's a pale-ass girl with white hair working in a biosafety cabinet in the big lab on the left. As I'm staring, she abruptly looks my way and glares at me through her safety goggles. I play like I'm inspecting the lab, put my arms behind my back and walk off casually.

Of course my dumb ass gets lost so I end up getting to the conference room with barely a minute to spare. The damn door squeals despite how slowly I pushed it open, prompting every person in the room to turn and stare. Dozer and Elsa shake their heads at me.

"Okay, I think that's everyone," O'Brian says. "Close the door behind you, please."

I do as I'm told and slink over to an empty seat in the corner.

"Before we begin, a little background about me," O'Brian says. "As most of you know, I go by the Vice. For those who don't know, yes, I am a big fucking deal. Before Richard Thomas came along, I belonged to Echelon, an elite group of soldiers headed by his brother Ryan. We uncovered Veritas and established the funds and the network that Richard used to build the Deciders. I'm the one who gave Richard the blueprint his brother left for him. I trained him, helped him plan out the Annex. He was like a little brother to me, so, needless to say, losing him hurt like hell.

"To be clear, I am *your* leader, but I am not *the* leader. In the absence of Richard, that is the Dominus, the highest-ranking member of Echelon. Everything that I have passed on to Richard came from him, just as everything I order you to do comes from him."

A map of the United States appears on the screen behind him along with a list of objectives:

- Infiltrate key positions in the government and defense forces.
- Establish new Hives under the guise of global reconstruction efforts.

- Recruit civilians sympathetic to Decider ideals.

- Locate Commander Anne Buckingham.

- Assassinate high-value targets who hinder progress.

- Identify and track the whereabouts of key AOW soldiers implicated in Richard Thomas's death.

- Bring down all governments before they solidify control.

A girl raises her hand. "Sorry, but the Ice Queen—do we know if she's still alive? And if she is, are we supposed to kill her? Is she a traitor?"

O'Brian turns his palms up. "According to founding member Major Don Chambers, the only survivor of the events leading to Richard's death, there was never any suspicion that she was working with the enemy. The working assumption is that she was captured sometime during the siege and coerced by the Angels of War to leave Norfolk defenseless for their attack. Our intel suggests that she is being held prisoner in a black site with other Decider POWs." He scans the room. "Any more questions?"

No one speaks.

"Based on your evaluations, skillsets, and service history," the Vice continues, "those of you in this room are among the few selected to help bring the Reclamation to fruition. You will be trained and educated for everything you'll need to complete every objective on the board. The Dominus stresses that we must identify and track the Angels of War responsible for overthrowing us before the Reclamation can begin."

A picture of a narrow-faced guy with deep-set eyes and long black hair appears on the screen. "To help us accomplish that, Corporal Andras Stevenson, a founding member of the Angels of War, will give you details on their personal relationships and highlight weaknesses you will be able to exploit. He'll teach you how they think and train you on their tactics. You will be meeting with him after we're done here. Any questions?"

There's silence.

"Excellent."

9

JEZEBEL

February 4

I ROAR THROUGH town on my snowmobile, passing low-slung building painted in cheerful colors. Yellow and black spotted seals hunker down on the ice in the harbor while the wind hurls sheets of snow.

When I'm not studying infiltration tactics and assassination techniques, training to jump out of airplanes, or enduring more torture resilience training, I spend as much time topside as I can, much of it in my little royal blue house right here in good ol' Qeqertarsuaq—Q-Town is what we call it. It's a nice escape from the subterranean life of Iceworm, though hardly a hermetic one. Elsa is always coming over to drink and watch movies. Dozer stops by a lot—and so does Owen, though I've managed to keep him out of my pants despite how much I've wanted to give in.

When I want to stretch my legs, I sign up for two-week stints on a boat called the *Kingfisher*, fishing for shrimp and cod in the bay. Being at sea brought me peace and reminded me of those times I went fishing along the Colorado River with my dad. I've even gone hiking on the ice cap with Elsa and the team a few times. I've come a long way from Texas but seeing how the desert was always trying to kill you too, it's not as big of an adjustment as you'd think. Just don't go outside when you're drunk, and watch out for crevasses.

The engine winds down as I park my ride under the white mylar tarp with the other snowmobiles. The snowdrift that blew under the canopy is ankle deep, nothing compared to the two feet beyond it. Bent over against the wind, I hurry to the door and press my thumb against the access panel. Once inside the mountain, I lift my fogging goggles, pull down the scarf wrapped around the lower half of my face, and smile at Sergeant Lehman, who's manning the security booth. Even Loyals not tasked with training or mission-critical work have to take shifts in admin, sanitation, and all that along with the rest of us. Cue a whole lot of bitching from this guy.

I stop at Locker 698 and press my thumb against the scanner to unlock it. It takes a bit of wiggling and shaking to shed my winter coat. I'm wearing thermals underneath my outerwear so I strip in the open then dress in the official uniform of the Enforcers—gray pants, black boots, and a burgundy trench coat—in preparation for today's event.

There's a flash of gray to my left as a stocky Loyal approaches his locker. Staff Sergeant Morton flashes a smile as he starts layering up.

"Hey, Peter," I say. "Not staying for the ceremony?"

"Nah, I got a ticket out of this arctic hell for a special assignment stateside. Time-sensitive shit." He grins, putting on his white winter hat. He's a real tech-savvy marksman who finished at the top of our hand-to-hand combat class, so it makes sense why he's shipping out early.

"Lucky ass," I say, closing the locker.

Boots dramatically stomp to a stop behind me. It's Andras. "From what I hear, you'll be leaving soon too," he says.

I fight the urge to roll my eyes. I mean, I'm glad he switched sides, and he's taught us a lot about the AOW, but he's kind of a dick. His stupid smirk, his insistence on wearing all black even when he's topside in the snow, and his long greasy hair makes me want to punch him in the face. Punch him again—I already did once when he tried getting handsy during a grappling class.

"Oh yeah?" I ask, putting on my best fake smile. "Thanks for the lowdown, Corporal."

"You know, I fought really hard to try and get you in my unit. It would have been nice having you around."

"I'm kind of glad it didn't work out," I say, slamming the locker shut. "I've got to get to the ceremony."

He tries brushing my cheek, but I dodge it. "I'll be seeing you around, Monroe."

I flash the peace sign then slowly transition to a middle finger, and he stomps out of the room.

"Good luck out there, nerd," I say to Peter.

He laughs. "Same to you, Isabella. Don't fuck up!"

"I'd never!" I say, shaking my head as I walk away.

Like tributaries joining a river, the hallways merge into a longer corridor as we stream toward the auditorium. I sit with my team. Slim Tim, Donovan, and the others at my rank are wearing our new uniform. So is Alma Bridwell, the noncombatant, Silicon Valley programmer who was flown to Iceworm with our group from Alaska. My bestie, Jason Dunn, was the only one of us to make Loyal. Like Elsa and Owen, he's dressed in all gray. Holt is wearing all white with forest green accents on the seams and around the pockets. A patch of a white bulldozer is stitched into his left shoulder. He's not Echelon class, as that rank is reserved for the Dominus's guild, but he's just below them and right above

Loyal. That means special gear and tech for him, like a friggin' helmet with a visor that lets you see through walls.

I raise my hand for a high five. "So it's official, you've been promoted to Elite! Congrats!"

Dozer's bear paw of a hand meets mine with a loud clap that burns my palm. "Hold up, were you doubting me, Lance Corporal Monroe?"

I wave him off. "Oh, I'd never do that Major Holt," I say in the southern accent that my aunt and my grandmother used to speak with.

The ceremony has gone on for longer than my high school graduation, and they funneled almost a thousand kids a year through that shithole. There was a speech about the future of the Deciders in a world post-Reclamation. Plans for future recruitment. Tactics we'll use to pit nations against each other. How we'll reclaim cities and towns. How to control the population after the *event* takes place. A video featuring plans for smart cities and centers for human advancement is shown. And just like a high school graduation, Dozer, Don Chambers, and other newly promoted Elites file on and off the stage to scattered bursts of applause. Then the newly promoted Loyals, then us Enforcers. We're given codenames, if we don't already have one, and graduation *gifts*.

Alma is the first up. She gets the codename Pixie, which is fitting because she's supposedly had a pixie cut since high school and Pixi3 was her internet handle on the deep web back when she was a hacker taking down government and student loan websites Pre-Annex. She was assigned to our team two weeks ago, but she's introverted as hell and doesn't talk much so that's all I really know about her.

An hour later, I finally take the stage.

"Lance Corporal Isabella Monroe," the Echelon soldier Rosa Ramirez says after taking my Nevron. She gives some praise, highlights my skills, and thanks me for my dedication to the cause like she has for everyone else. Then she hands me a new device that's flatter than the Nevron and has a larger screen. "This is your Gauntlet. From this day forward, you will serve the Deciders under the codename Jezebel. May you dedicate the rest of your days to establishing peace through unity and truth." As a parting gift, she gives me a Velcro nametag that has my new codename on it.

When it's all over, we break off into our individual units. I flop in a chair next to Elsa, bitter as all hell. "Jezebel? So they think I'm a slut, huh? I'm guessing you had something to do with this."

"But of course," she says. "Anyway, I meant it as a compliment."

I snort. "How is branding me a morally unrestrained woman a compliment? How's this going to play into my role in the Deciders from here on out?"

The door ahead of us opens and the ginger general signals for us to come in.

Elsa slaps her legs and rises. "You're about to find out."

The room holds the exact number of people in our unit—fifty. A woman with short hair and an Elite with some kind of monster symbol on his arm walk through the rows and hand out folders.

General O'Brian gets right to it. "Do I have a treat for the Dozer crew!" he says, pointing a finger gun at Holt. "Your performance pre-Iceworm and during your time here has landed you an assignment at the tip of the fuckin' spear for the Reclamation!"

Dozer pumps a fist. Elsa grins at me and I smirk back, even though that makes me nervous.

"We're shipping you to Baltimore, where you will take root and prepare for Operation Omega Anax. No details of the operation will be provided until the time comes, but for now, your mission is as follows: Recruit sympathizers to our mission. Establish a Hive using the construction company we have established. Collect intel from the targets we send you, USAW and otherwise. Eliminate targets that pose a threat to the mission."

While the Vice continues lecturing on the finer points of the mission, the Loyal girl hands me a folder with my name on it. Inside I find a passport, a driver's license, cash, credit cards, and a personal mission file. The identity I will be assuming is Daisy Belle. I wrinkle my nose—that was my stripper name. She has my birthday and her background is about same as mine—a psych student with years of experience with dancing. Daisy's one-upped me by holding a certification as a contemporary dance instructor, which is awesome because it's something I'd wanted to do after completing a long career as a professional dancer. My specific mission instructions include recruiting, inserting myself into social circles that can get me in good with targets, and "seducing male targets by any means for the purposes of assassinating them, accessing mission-critical computer networks, sabotaging key structures, and collecting intel." In other words, sexpionage …

My cheeks get hot. Sure, I like sex a lot, but I only bang dudes I like. I signed up to fight, not to be a goddamn escort!

I lean into Crawford. "The shit is this? You're whoring me out?" That last bit comes out a little louder than I intended. Dozer glares at me and O'Brian side-eyes me.

"Shut it!" Crawford whispers. "We'll talk after."

After the meeting, everyone heads to Dozer's place, one of the larger two-story homes in the center of town. I walk in silence at the rear of the pack, head down and hands in my pockets. I feel dirty and I didn't even do anything yet.

Elsa falls back and grabs my arm. "You're not a whore," she says. "And we're not your pimps. You're just a natural at this, that's all."

"A natural at what?"

"Oh, give me a break. You were a stripper—"

"And I quit."

"And a camgirl—"

"And I never fucked anybody for that."

Elsa stops. "And you never fucked anybody to get what you want? You fucked that Uber driver so he'd look after—"

"That's not why I slept with him," I say.

"Fine, so he wouldn't hate you. And what about when you cheated on Zach with some choreographer for a shot at that dance team? You screwed around with that guy for a month even though he kept casting other girls for the spots you wanted!"

My eyes are watering now. "Is this supposed to be some kind of pep talk? If it is, you can stop now because it fucking sucks."

Her eyes narrow. "Don't you talk to your superior that way."

I turn my head and roll my eyes, wiping away the tears that fall before they freeze to my cheek. "I'm sorry, ma'am."

"You're not a whore, you're a weapon of mass seduction. You use your sex appeal as a weapon and you'll go as far as you damn well please to get what you want. And you've never done anything with anyone that you didn't want to. And now you have the skills to take handle any sonofabitch who tries to take advantage of you. So don't you get pissy with me for setting you up for a role you'll shine in. Got it?"

All the sexually manipulative things I've done come back to me in a hazy wave of alcohol-blurred memories. My second semester of college, I drunkenly hooked up with a friend's boyfriend just because I was lonely and I knew he was into me. Our friendship ended when she found out a few weeks later … Following that, there were those two really nice guys that I'd always tease by sitting on their laps and giving them over the pants rubs at parties just to keep them lusting after me—to keep them buying me coffee and food. One week before Zach found out I was banging the choreographer, I gave a BJ to a popular DJ named TyDie in the bathroom after he invited me on stage … and then I hooked up with him at his penthouse the weekend after. Sure, he was super-hot, but I was really after all the exclusive clubs and parties he could get me into, places where I could meet someone important and get hired as a model or dancer. The funny thing is that I got into all of the biggest events in LA over the last few months and never met anyone worthwhile …

More often than not, I blamed alcohol for my promiscuous, immoral, unfaithful behavior. But the truth is, ninety percent of the time, I left the house with the intent to do all those crappy things because I like sex and I have fun doing scandalous shit sometimes. And maybe I think monogamy is outdated. Getting sloppy drunk beforehand was just a copout to shift the blame to my boozed-up alter ego Bella because that was easier than admitting to myself that I wasn't the good girl society said I had to be.

I exhale deeply after taking a long hard look at my life, my decisions. "No, you're right."

"Good," she says, looping her arm under mine. "You are Jezebel, a shameless woman unrestrained by social norms. You will do what you have to make the Reclamation happen. Because you want to, not because we demand it. Remember that."

10
HIVES

March 1

THE WAR-DAMAGED buildings of Boston's skyline come into view as we make our approach. I stand at the bow of the *Kingfisher* beside Dozer, leaning against the rail as a bone-chilling wind stings our faces. I'm layered up with a wool sweater, a navy-blue coat, gray mountain climbing pants, and long underwear. The other members of Advent Squad are dressed in fisherman getups as well. The fur at the edge of my hood dances violently in my peripheries as I pull my scarf up to my nose. As the gap closes between our bobbing vessel and the ruins, cranes and scaffolding begin taking shape.

I wonder how many of those construction companies are Decider fronts …
As we near the docks, three boats appear ahead.

"Stay frosty, Advent." Owen, or Shawshank, announces from the cabin. Pretty much every Decider but me has always called him Bradshaw, and that's been shortened to Shaw over time. Apparently, he's crazy good with knives and during his deployment in Texas, a mission gone awry led to him being stuck behind enemy lines with nothing but a pair of combat knives that he used to stab his way to extraction. That feat earned him the nickname Shawshank, and that's what he was dubbed during the ceremony at Iceworm. "We've got three USAW boats coming right for us."

"Copy," Dozer says. "They're definitely gonna board us. Everybody stay chill and we'll be good."

"It's twenty degrees," I mutter, teeth chattering. "Kinda hard not to stay frosty and chill in this weather."

"Shut it, Jezebel. I said be chill, not cheesy."

The black and blue boats surround us. Sailors dressed in navy blue combat jackets with black stripes down the sleeve and black pants stand at attention, rifles in hand. "As mandated by Annex Act 867," the lead sailor begins, "we are required by the United States of the Americas to search any and all vessels in our waters not equipped with authorized oceanic vessel transponders and we are required to check all occupants' papers before allowing passage. If you do not comply, we will have no choice to board with extreme prejudice."

It's the Americas now because the US annexed Central and South America, the West Indies, and Puerto Rico in the power vacuum our fall left behind. Canada, Japan, and the Philippines are supposedly next. With Russia, China, and the Islamic states doing the same, the world's in a worse place than it was before the war— the elites we tried to cast down have seized and consolidated even more power.

"Come on up!" Dozer shouts.

One of the men tosses us a rope ladder. Dozer hooks it onto the railing and the USAW sailors board us like pirates. It takes everything not to let the bitterness and disdain for these men show on my face as they climb aboard. Our Echelon trainers drilled it into us that Dion Johnson is the epitome of everything wrong with humanity. He took to the battlefield to keep mankind in shackles and made it his mission to exterminate us just like Hitler did with the Jews. If there's anyone who can attest to this, it's Andras Stevenson, who planned attacks with Johnson and fought beside him. And he confirmed the profile on Dark Angel was all accurate. Though Johnson has gone underground to hide from his monstrous crimes, the US Angels of War and the next wave of elites have reclaimed power in his name. Everything he is or was now lives on in those who were inspired by his actions and in those who have read that six-hundred-page piece of propaganda he wrote called *War of Annex*. Everyone who has enlisted in his name is the enemy.

Their lead sailor asks for our papers and passports. Dozer radios everyone to come up on deck with their identification.

"Where are you all coming from?" the sailor asks.

"Up near Newfoundland," Holt responds.

"You from the States?"

Holt nods. "Jersey, born and raised."

"Why don't you have a transponder?"

"We left before they were issued. Had some trouble getting back in time due to inclement weather."

The members of Advent squad start lining up. Owen hands the USAW sailor a stack of our documentation. The admiral shuffles through them. "Alright. While I look over these, my men will search your vessel for stowaways and contraband."

Dozer nods. "Daisy, you and Omar go with them and open up anything they need to see."

The sailor scans Owen's and my passports with his tablet. "These two check out."

Of course we do ... We've got friends in your government uploading our aliases.

"Right this way, gentlemen," I say to the four men who assemble in front of us. We take them to the cabin first. They search every compartment, banging on walls and checking for loose floor panels. They even dig into our ice chests full of smelt, and I do my best to hold a pleasant smile as one sailor's getting closer to the false bottom concealing the grenades beneath it.

I lean against the crate the more handsome sailor is inspecting and rest my chin in my palm. "So, what's your name?" I ask.

"McSorley," he says.

I flutter my eyelashes. "There's a joke in there, yeah? You like to leave them sore?"

"Oh, I've seen some action," he says, not understanding the entendre. "But I was a civilian back then. Fought at sea with some sailors who survived the early days of the Annex. We torpedoed the *Crucible*, killed a thousand of those bastards. Some of them are still washing up onshore when the currents are right. Fish didn't leave much of them intact though." He moves to the next crate, one that's a little less covered up than the previous one.

"Ooh, I like a man who knows how to fire his torpedo," I say, trying my best to not sound disgusted. "I've always had a thing for seamen."

He looks up, having finally caught on. "Oh, yeah? How long are you in town? They just reopened Pier 6 if you're into oysters and … uh … seamen." He laughs. "My apologies, I'm immature."

I pretend to trip and fall into him, brushing my breast against his bicep as I laugh. "I'm no better! What time do you want to meet up?"

"I dunno, eleven?" he asks. He's blushing now as he stands up to walk away.

"Why don't you finish checking that crate before you run off to jerk it to that siren?" the other sailor asks.

McSorley pivots back around, even redder than before. "I'll check again if it makes you feel better." He shoves his hand back in, hits something, and makes a face.

I look to Owen then look back to McSorley. "You get bit by a fish, sailor?" I ask as he begins scooping away ice.

"Your fish made of metal?"

Owen gives me the signal and I snatch McSorley's gun and crack him over the head with it. Shawshank slices the throat of the sailor nearest to him then stabs him in the heart before darting over to the door. He presses his back against the wall, lets the first guy come through, and stabs the second one while the first is distracted by me waving him over for help. When he turns at the sound of his comrade gagging, I knife him in the back and kick him behind the knees, then plunge the knife into his neck.

McSorley's up on his knees, groaning and rubbing his head. "You bastards are Deciders, aren't you?" he asks.

I smile. "Nope, we're pirates."

Owen grabs him by the hair and holds a knife to his throat. "Tell your boss that it's all clear down here and I won't gut you like a fish. Okay?" He cuts his neck a little.

"Alright! Easy! Easy!" He toggles on his radio. "McSorley checking in. We're all clear down here. Over."

"Good copy. Their papers check out. Clearing them with the docks now. Over."

The transmission is cut.

McSorley shakes his head. "Whatever it is you're planning, you won't get away with it. We'll stop you"

Owen slices through his throat.

I tap my Gauntlet. "Things got messy down here so I'll have to clean up. You might want to do the same topside."

There are no USAW sailors left standing by the time we get above deck. Owen and I get right to work dragging bodies toward the bow.

Elsa's cleaning off her knife on some dude's uniform. "What did you two do?"

Owen gestures at me. "She told him that she likes seamen and he realized that no girl is that slutty so she must be a Decider …"

I punch him in the arm. "Shut up, Owen … Remember that big ass container we were worried about? Yeah, they found it under the salmon …"

"Doesn't matter." Dozer says. "We're clear to dock so let's send these men off."

We piled the corpses onto their boats and sent them out to sea at full throttle after our resident voice imitator, Nicholas, radioed in to say they were going to pursue some suspicious activity. Their boats were rigged to blow in a few hours so we won't have to worry about anyone finding the fileted USAW Coastguard and raising any flags.

At the port, we haul our gear off of the *Kingfisher* and pile it into the refrigerated food truck a different Decider cell left for us in the parking lot along with some SUVs. A few miles into the drive, I start nodding in and out of sleep. The next thing I know, I wake up as we park behind an old warehouse.

"Where are we?" I groan.

"Northern Pennsylvania. Milford," Dozer says, checking his Gauntlet. "We're meeting up with the rest of our team before heading to our new home."

Nodding, I look to my Gauntlet and double-tap the map to expand it. It's in 3D, a white-lined grid of the building on a black background. Inside the warehouse on both floors are yellow blips. Most are circle shaped, denoting low-ranked soldiers such as myself. The stars are the Elites and select high-ranked Loyals. If there were trespassers broadcasting known enemy signals within the range of a TARSEN (Total Area Sensory) field, they would show up as red blips. Anyone with a cellphone or a civilian radio would show up as gray blips. And if that isn't enough, the TARSEN field lets any Elite with a Farsight camera–embedded Deva helmet see through walls. It will definitely tilt things in our favor come the next war …

ADVENT SQUAD IS CLEAR TO ENTER appears on the screen. The bay door opens and our SUV rolls in, the rest of the convoy following behind us. Soldiers dressed in civilian clothes are scattered throughout the warehouse. Even their civilian getups are in one of the three Decider colors of burgundy, white, or gray. We exit our vehicles and get to work unloading our gear into the trucks they have waiting for us.

"Took you guys long enough!" Slim Tim says as he and Dunn, who's now his team leader, rise from a cafeteria table. Tim takes the box I'm hauling away from me.

"Thanks," I say. "Sorry, traveling by sea isn't as quick as flying."

"Get into any trouble?" Kappa asks.

"No, but the Coastguard did," I say.

When everything is in place, the boys take me on a tour of the Hive. Supposedly this one is on the smaller side, serving more as a refueling point where people change rides and lie low for a bit before moving on. Still, the command center is as fancy as anything in Iceworm. We'll be here for the night so I take my things into the bathroom to shower and change into something a little more stylish and a little less *Deadliest Catch*.

March 2

The Dawnbreaker platoon starts out at one A.M., leaving in twenty-minute intervals. My group left around two so we reach the ruins of Baltimore just after first light. While Boston was in the process of rebuilding, this place looks like it was besieged hundreds of years ago and no one dared come back to rebuild. There are no people on the streets. Some roads are still impassible from crumbled buildings, abandoned cars, blast craters, and fallen helicopters.

We park in front of 300 North Charles Street, a pretty red-brick apartment building with papered-over storefronts on the ground floor.

"Everything between Saratoga Street to East Pleasant is ours," Dozer says.

"Maybe we can reopen that bar and use it as a front," I say.

Elsa snorts. "Oh yeah, and maybe you and I can start a Baltimore version of *Coyote Ugly* …"

Dozer turns down the alley and swings around to the parking garage out back that's blocked off by a metal gate covered in graffiti brandishing the Angels of War Militia logo. The sight of it makes me gag … I'm thinking I might have to come out here later and spray paint over it.

With a few taps of his Gauntlet, Holt gets the gate to rise remotely then the convoy pulls in. There are a few trucks inside and some vehicles covered by tarps, plus a dozen or so blackened wrecks scattered about to make our fleet less conspicuous. Dozer puts on his Farsight helmet while Elsa, Tim, and I plant a few TARSEN emitters.

"Friendlies inside still have heartbeats," Dozer says. His voice comes out clear like he's not wearing a helmet at all. He punches in our code to the keypad next to the door and we head down into the basement, our Hive.

All of the buildings above are connected below ground by doorways blasted through walls. There are offices, a command center, a room with lockers for an armory, and a few bunks. On my Gauntlet, TARSEN scans of the Hive show that there are fellow Deciders in the buildings above, probably settling in the apartments they selected. This Hive can fit all of us and probably a hundred more.

Elsa sighs. "This place is a hell of a lot better than Iceworm, that's for damn sure."

"Needs a home makeover, though," I say.

"We'll be here for more than a year," Dozer says, "so how about we get this place functional and secure before we start going all HGTV?"

11
HONEYPOT

October 16

THE BARTENDER POURS me another glass of Cabernet blanc and flashes me a smile. "Let me know if you need anything else."

I smile back. "Keep an eye out, hon. I'll be needing ya real soon."

As I sip from my glass, I watch the other patrons. Compared to most bars, Brewvine Tavern here in Columbia, Maryland, is one of the more decent ones in the area. It's evident that, unlike the people I usually see in the Baltimore dive bars I frequent, these people have some semblance of class. The guys are in button downs, khakis, pea coats, loafers, dress shoes and all that. The women are in dresses, despite the chilly fall weather.

There's a couple on a date at the table nearest me. It's clear by their body language and their conversation that it's a first date. They both have sad eyes and look like they're trying to find something in each other that they lost. A group of four friends who are rowdier than everyone else are throwing back shots at the table over my shoulder. At the bar, three loners sit one chair apart from each other and watch the TV in silence. Unlike the others who play at having a good time, unlike those who are smugly pretending they are victors of a war that no one truly one, those sad saps aren't hiding their pain with laughs.

The war has taken something vital from so many people. It's sad really, what the Annex has done to those who came out of the other side without their jobs, loved ones, and homes. There is no doubt that the nation as a whole is hurting based on the spikes in alcohol sales. I hear strip clubs are booming too … And so is street crime, especially in cities, thanks to the economic lull that followed the Architect's incomplete societal reboot. I've seen teenagers fleeing homes with sacks of stolen property in broad daylight numerous times while driving through the city and watched almost a dozen live news reports of police standoffs with robbers holding up banks and supermarkets. Hell, I almost got mugged at like one in the afternoon a few weeks ago. It goes without saying that he pulled a knife on the wrong girl …

"Target inbound, Jezebel," Elsa says through my earpiece.

I turn right, brushing my curls from my face as he walks in. Jackson Zeigler is an average-looking guy with a dad bod. He's dressed in a light blue dress shirt, khakis, and brown shoes. Trendy designer glasses of some kind rest on his face. His hair isn't much shorter than mine. Somehow he looks both suave and geeky at the same time. And I kind of dig it. Of all the Machina Cybersecurity Systems Inc. employees that we surveilled, he was the only mark looking for love on a dating app. At least the only one who would likely fall for a honeypot.

Since DC was cratered by the antimatter bomb, a lot of the big cybersecurity companies began cropping up in southern Maryland and northern Virginia. And a lot of their employees, like Mr. Zeigler over there, tend to visit places like this after a long day's work of defending the business and news media world from people like little ol' me. He stands near the entrance talking to the hostess for a bit before looking around for the girl he met online. And that girl isn't coming. Or I guess she's already here? To bait him, Pixie used some picture editing software to render a profile picture for a girl that looks eerily similar to the girlfriend he lost during the Annex. Of course he matched with her. So, for the last few weeks, I've been catfishing him.

He scans bar and eventually makes eye contact with me. I flash him a faint smile and take a sip of wine, turning my head down to my phone. I don't have to look up to check if he's coming over. I'm dressed just the way the nonexistent girl he's looking to meet said she'd be—I've got on a tight, navy-blue dress and I'm wearing glasses. I even straightened my hair and got extensions to look more like the profile picture we used.

"Jennifer?" he asks.

I turn to him, pushing away my hair again. "Michelle ..." I say with an apprehensive smile.

The guy gets all flustered. "Sorry, you look like someone I'm supposed to be meeting."

"That's what you get for showing up early," I joke, turning my smirk into a welcoming smile.

He sighs. "I'm actually late ..."

"She's standing you up?"

"It wouldn't be the first time ..."

I snort. "She was probably just intimidated by a smart looking stud like you."

"I guess." He takes a step back like he's about to walk away.

"My friends bailed on me too. Why don't I buy you drink while you see if this chick can summon up the nerve?"

"You sure?"

I slide out a barstool with my foot. He sits. "Jackson," he says, extending a hand. I'm weirded out by how soft it is when we shake. He clears his throat and orders a whiskey sour from the bartender.

As I gleaned from his profile and a brief exchange of banter, Jackson's not an asshole or a creep, which makes things both easier and harder. Like, he was on the phone with his girlfriend of four years while she was stuck on the George Washington Bridge in New York City when it blew. There was an explosion, rumbling, her shrill screams, crashing sounds, and then the sound of water rushing into the car. She died along with countless others when Richard Thomas gave the order to demolish the bridges and tunnels surrounding all major cities to keep people from evacuating. It's hard to stomach, but it was a necessary war crime I'm choosing to overlook since our endgame will save billions of lives. And now this is going to play out however I choose it to. Jackson caught a bad break winding up with me, but that's what he gets for opposing the Deciders.

I tell him that I teach at a dance studio, which isn't a lie. It's been Daisy Belle's cover job for the last few months where I've been recruiting Decider-minded girls. I also recruit guys and girls from bars and demonstrations. But that's not what this is.

We laugh and joke, and I find reasons to hit him, touch his arm and hand, and lean into him with my tits. Eventually, he starts building up some small level of confidence.

"Is it weird to say that I'm happy that I was stood up?" he asks.

"Not at all. Is it horrible of me that I'm glad you were?"

"A little …" he says with a smile.

I give a little shove. "Oh, whatever!"

He eyes his smartwatch. "You didn't drive here, did you?"

"Why do you ask?"

He blushes. "Oh, you seem too buzzed to drive so I was just going to offer to get you an Uber!"

"You planning on sending me home or were you going to lure me back to your place?" I ask. He starts to stammer, and I stop him with a hand to his birdcage of a chest. "I'm just kidding. You don't seem like a serial killer. Let's go."

As Jackson pays the bartender, I see … of all people … Austin?

"Something wrong?" Jackson asks.

"I think I see one of my friends … Excuse me for a moment, okay?"

I bump through the people standing near the bar, wondering how Austin might have ended up here. Maybe he joined the rebellion and came east to enlist in USAW. Maybe he ended up back with the Deciders in an attempt to find me.

I put my hand on his shoulder and he turns around. Sadness washes through me when I realize it isn't him. "Oh, sorry! I thought you were a friend of mine."

Austin's slightly more handsome doppelganger smiles cockily as he checks me out. "I can be your friend if you wanted, beautiful."

"If I wasn't already with someone, I'd take you up on that," I say, then make my way back to the bar.

Once I get my jacket, Jackson and I head to his BMW. The entire time he's talking, I'm too distracted to respond how I should. Austin is the only thing on my mind.

"You okay?" Jackson asks.

"Getting a little hungry is all."

Back at his apartment, he pops some frozen perogies in the oven while I peruse his alcohol supply. He's got IPAs and stout in the fridge and whiskey and vodka on a shelf above his wine rack.

"Sooo how about we do a few shots and down some beers?" I ask, grabbing the bottle of Johnny Walker.

"I'm game!" Jackson says. He grabs a pair of shot glasses from the cabinet.

We throw back the shots and then I pour another round.

"Let me use the bathroom right quick," he says.

"You puke and I leave!" I tease as he walks across the room.

The door closes, and the moment I hear pee blast toilet water, I wipe the smile off my face and rifle through my purse until I find the liquid drug disguised as mouthwash. I dump some of his shot down the garbage disposal and top it off with the solution. I get two bottles of beer out and set them beside the shots.

When Jackson returns, he takes his shot and chases it with the beer, as do I. The drug is called Morpheus. It is tasteless and odorless so the burn of the liquor is the only thing he reacts to. We sit on the couch afterward, my legs crossed and my feet resting on his lap, toes caressing his thigh. About thirty minutes pass. He mumbles something about drinking too fast then his head drops and he's out. Morpheus is a benzodiazepine stronger than roofies that also leaves victims with anterograde amnesia, meaning memory leading up to being dosed gets wiped. He'll probably be out until noon tomorrow, but at least he won't die like the last target I had to seduce ...

I lift his lifeless arm from my leg and then swipe his phone. "Target's down for the count. Standby for upload."

"Copy that," Elsa says over the radio.

I turn on his Bluetooth, set my phone beside his on the counter and activate the app. While it clones his device, I search his place for his work badge, laptop, and work phone. The work computer was in the laptop bag he hauled in and hid under his bed. It's something we've watched him bring home every night. The badge was with it and so was the phone. Using the card reader, I copy the badge's encryption then use a handheld scanner to copy it so we can make duplicates. Then I clone the work phone and install an app that will give us access to Machina's internet and intranet. Pixie remotes into both his laptop and work iPhone then installs programs that will give us backdoor access to their systems.

"Alright, Jez," Pixie radios. "We're good to go."

"Copy," I say, splashing some Frank's Red Hot on the perogies before wrapping them in a cone of foil. I'm hungry as hell and I don't want his apartment to catch fire. After putting everything back where I found it, I write him a little note:

Looks like you couldn't hang. Too bad, you missed out on a good time. Thanks for the perogies!

—Michelle

October 18

After turning up the radio, I take a long sip of my pumpkin spice latte and look to the clock in my maroon Subaru Crosstrek. It's 13:10. I've been sitting in this abandoned parking lot for the past two hours waiting for Owen to complete his mission. My bladder's about to burst so I'm contemplating taking a page out of drunk Isabella's book and pissing right outside.

Using the backdoor in Jackson's computer, we were able to hack into the Machina Cybersecurity Systems security network and give Owen an employee profile as a mid-level IT guy. The badge Pixie made for him gave him access to the building and the secure areas of the company, including the server room. Machina Inc. forbids its employees from bringing in personal electronics, and everything beyond the lobby is what Pixie called a SCIF, or a Sensitive Compartmented Information Facility. She dumbed it down for me, saying that a SCIF is basically an area where no signals can get in or out of, except for work specific devices that are connected to their secured internet. Guess that means I've just got to wait and see whether Owen pulls off this mission. And he better too. Machina Inc. provides next-gen encryption for internet and cable providers, smartphones, and the power grid—crucial points of control that we need to take over if the Reclamation is going to come to fruition …

Another twenty minutes pass before a shitty Nissan Altima rounds the corner and pulls up beside me.

I roll down the window. "About damn time, Shawshank! I gotta pee!"

Owen climbs out of the car and goes to the back seat to grab his gear. "Ain't no one around. You could've squatted in the bushes and watered the grass like the classy girl you are."

I roll my eyes. "How'd it go?"

"No complications," he says, climbing into my passenger seat. "We're good to go whenever we get the green light."

I back up and head down the gravel road. "Dope."

"The world won't know what hit it."

"Everything's so compartmentalized, even we don't know what's gonna happen."

"Speak for yourself." Owen's face goes serious. "When the Reclamation kicks off, every person in the world is going to wish the Angels of War didn't intervene the last time."

12

RECLAMATION'S DAWN

September 4, One Year Later

THE HOTEL ROOM door opens slowly and Jonathon Prescott enters, checking all corners before closing the door behind him.

I lean back on the bed, resting on my elbows as I bite my lip and spread my legs, giving him a clear view up my skirt.

A naughty smile creeps onto his face as he removes his cap and throws it onto the armchair. "Oh, I've missed you, babe."

"Sorry, I've been a little busy," I say. "Don't worry—no client work, just traveling."

"And I'm the first guy you messaged since clocking back in?"

I stand up and give him a kiss. "Of course you are, Jonny."

He lifts me up and I wrap my legs around him, letting him carry me to the bed.

Oh, the things I have done to this man to keep him coming back for the past few months. Oh, the things I've done just to get to him. It took a couple of jobs with three other important government and military types for me to make it onto this buster's radar as a high-end escort. Like the other industries these days dealing in vices, the escort business is booming, especially since it's been legalized and regulated. There's a lot of competition out there, but the agency I inserted myself into is top tier and deals with the specific clientele this mission requires me to get close to. The first move to getting to my target required me to be arm candy for a pious yet lonely congressman who needed a date for a political fundraising gig hosted by the Angels of Earth nonprofit organization. That night, I marketed my services to the targets we found to be most likely to hire gals like me, stooges who worked in private security and often interacted with Jonathon professionally and used the same escort service. A few sexual favors later, I managed to use a sleeping client's phone to recommend myself to the special agent who's currently sliding his hand up under my skirt.

"FOUND A SMOKE SHOW YOU HAVE TO TRY OUT, JON! BOOK HER FOR TWO NIGHTS USING THIS LINK AND GET THE SECOND NIGHT 75% OFF. TOTALLY WORTH IT!" was the deal. That horny bastard requested an appointment with me an hour later.

Prescott is a former military man who fought during the Disintegration, the final series of battles of the Annex. Now he works as a Secret Service agent for the man he rescued, Vice President Gary Lewis. The profile on Jonathon suggested that he is emotionally detached and too busy with work to form a relationship so he tends to stick to hookups or paid sex. And of course when the Deciders needed a weapon of mass seduction to exploit this flaw and get to him, I'm the one they sent in.

He tosses my dress across the room. While he kisses me from my neck to my crotch, I take out the syringe from underneath the pillow. I crawl back to the headboard and summon him forward with a finger. He fumbles with his belt, slides on a condom, and almost dives onto the mattress. As his mouth finds my neck, I grab him by the hair, stab the needle into his neck, and depress the plunger.

His hand grabs my wrist and pins it to the bed while the other yanks the syringe out. "What the fuck!" he shouts, grabbing my throat. "You bitch! What the hell is this!"

Gagging, I strike his throat with the space between my thumb and index finger, leaving him coughing and gasping for air. When his grip breaks, I put him in a chokehold. He tries to fight me off, but the Morpheus tranquilizer puts him out in seconds.

I roll his body off of me and I lie there panting for a moment, cringing at the phantom sensations of his touch that still linger all over my body. *That was the last time you'll have to do that,* I tell myself.

I tug the duffle bag containing a change of clothes out from under the bed and put in my earpiece. "Jonny Boy is napping," I say as I pull on my jeans.

"Copy that," Owen responds. "Did you use the drugs or did you ride him into a coma?"

That's the kind of bitter ass comment I usually get from him after "missions" like these. There's no doubt that he's salty that I'm screwing all these strangers yet still won't be the warm body he yearns to lay with at night.

My black hoodie goes on next. "Shut the hell up and get your bitch ass over here, Shawshank."

"Alright, alright! Sorry. We're on the way up."

When Dunn and Owen arrive dressed like housekeeping staff, we shove Prescott into a laundry cart and bury him under sheets and the clothes he and I shed. Dunn doesn't even look at me once the whole time. I don't blame him. I've been shitty to him as of late and he finally got tired of trying to being a good friend to me.

As we wheel Prescott out, Pixie plays a loop of the empty hall and garage footage on the hacked CCTV.

"We taking him back to the Hive?" I ask.

Owen shakes his head. "This one is going straight to Naraka."

From what I know, Naraka is a black site where turncoats, government officials, and captured enemies go for who knows what. I don't ask about it because it doesn't really matter to me. Nothing really matters much to me these days …

I climb into the car parked beside the van. "Gotcha. See you back at base."

Owen looks me over. "You coming to watch the show with us tomorrow?"

I shake my head. "I just need some me time." I slam the door, start the engine, and pull out before they're even in the car.

I arrive at the Hive forty minutes later. When I get to my apartment, I pound two glasses of whiskey and then head for the bathroom. I stand in the shower under the hard-spraying hot water in a daze. I collapse onto my ass with my knees clutched to my chest and sob. When the water turns cold, I get up and start scrubbing myself. Like every time after I have to whore myself out, I scrub until it hurts, desperately trying to get the filth off. But you can't wash away the self-disgust, not with soap or by drowning yourself with alcohol. I know because I've tried. I don't know how many bottles I've killed in the last few months.

I've murdered people. I surrendered my body up to strangers just to lure in one guy to get tortured and probably killed. And for what? Everything is so damn compartmentalized, I don't even know what I'm fighting or fucking for anymore.

Cold and dripping wet, I stand before the mirror staring at my reddened skin before looking into my own eyes. Why me? Of all the women in the Deciders, why do I have to play a prostitute? Am I just that worthless? Is that all I'm on this earth for, to be used as a source of pleasure?

You did webcam porn, remember? the bitchier version of my voice says in my head. You used sex to manipulate men for money, and favors. You were a stripper. You were too free with your body and the universe took notice.

What would your father think of you now?

I should have run off with Austin. We probably wouldn't have made it out, but at least I'd be dead.

September 5

I've spent the whole day in bed, only getting up to make myself some mac and cheese. It tasted like shit but I've been sucking in so much weed and guzzling so much wine that my stomach was going to turn on me if I didn't eat something solid. Also, I've got a real bad case of the munchies.

My Gauntlet vibrates. It's a message from Elsa: "Showtime! Where are you?!"

I text back: "I'm not feeling well. Watching in bed." Then I grab the remote and put on CNN. She replies, but I ignore it. I'm sure she knows that something's up with me. If I'm not at my cover job between "missions," I avoid the Hive. And when I go out, Pixie is usually the only Decider I spend time with. She's the only one I don't resent for putting me through this bullshit.

Out of everyone in Advent Squad who I kind of cut off, Dunn took it the most personal. As he should. Though I'm sure he would have totally been down for ten minutes of passion with me, we were best friends. But the bastard doesn't even talk to me in passing or acknowledge my presence these days. As if I needed to feel anymore worthless than I already do …

No one told me what the big show was supposed to be. I just know that it will serve as the kickoff for everything we've been working toward. When I see President Pell on screen to give a special Labor Day Address to the Nation, I put two and two together and drain my glass of wine. The poor guy doesn't know what's about to hit him.

Pell blabs on about how America and all the nations it snapped up are growing toward an ideal nation. "It's not the government that's responsible for the recent economic boom and the nation's recovery. It's the American workforce—the American spirit."

"Bullshit!" my drunk ass yells at the TV. "We're rebuilding this country! You just don't know it yet!"

Then something blows up on screen, making me jump. The blast leaves the camera crooked. Bullets start flying, blood starts spraying, and bodies start dropping. Deciders dressed in masks storm the stage and effortlessly pick off Secret Service agents. Two guys force Pell onto his knees, holding him in place. A third soldier walks up behind him, draws a pistol, and pulls the trigger. I pump my fist and take a deep drag out of my bowl. Fucking assholes.

The world thought the Deciders were dead and gone. Little do they know that all those supposedly random deaths of government officials around the world were our doing. They don't know that the attack on Coeus Labs three days ago wasn't just a means to capture the best scientists in the country, it was also a personal attack against the CEO, Dion Johnson. It turns out that he didn't just steal Richard Thomas's money, he's also been gaining wealth from pawning off our scientific advancements as his own. Today marks the countdown to what we've been calling Reclamation's Dawn, the kickoff for what sounds like will be the last war humanity will ever have to fight. I reach past my wine, grab my water bottle, and start chugging. I'll need to get my shit together soon before they call on me.

13
OMEGA ANAX

September 9

TWO DAYS AGO, the mission that involved me seducing Jackson Zeigler, the analyst from Machina Cybersecurity Systems finally paid off. We hacked every streaming site and TV channel in the world, allowing our new leader, the Dominus, to let the world know that the Deciders were alive and well.

Like Richard Thomas, the man in white kept his identity a secret from the world. The difference with this guy is that most of us still don't even know who the hell he is ... Following a faceless leader kind of sketches me out, but it's not like I can stop now. There's no safe way of jumping off the train once it starts chugging along, just like my dad used to say. I can't go back to my mom or sister until the world belongs to the Deciders. There's no going back to a normal life because defecting will land me in Naraka ... if it doesn't get me killed.

All I have is this mission.

I am our mission.

Things are in full gear now. Since Pell's death, dozens of other empty suits have been killed by my brothers and sisters overseas. The world powers in Europe, Africa, Russia, and the Middle East took it with all the equanimity you would expect, mobilizing their armies and threatening each other with annihilation. Short chubby men ranting in front identical-looking soldiers isn't something you just see in North Korea anymore. Chaos is spreading and the world is teetering on conflict, just the way it is supposed to be. Whether we incited it or not, this outcome was inevitable. World war is always the endgame when it comes to rivaling nations with agendas.

So far as America goes, we have two spies, Corax and Corvus, embedded into the Angels of War. Apparently, President Lewis and the rest of their top rats are trying to flee to some mountain base in Pennsylvania. And thanks to the information that was tortured out of Special Agent Jonathon Prescott, we know the exact route that they'll take. And thanks to his help, we're tapped into their communications too. Couldn't have done it without me, which makes me hate myself a little less.

Richmond is in much better shape than Baltimore, which means its streets look like they had had a hideous case of acne rather than smallpox. Our convoy turns onto Byrd Street and pulls up to a windowless concrete-walled factory on a strip of land between the James River and the Richmond City canal. This is the site of another major Decider Hive.

"Welcome to the major leagues, Dawnbreaker," Dozer announces over the radio to the platoon as our convoy pulls rolls through the cargo bay door.

Of the four people who approach us, I recognize two: Don Chambers and that rat bastard Andras Stevenson. Don's in gray instead of white; Andras is in black as usual. I slink back into the group, trying to stay hidden as they lead us to the stairwell.

"Told ya I'd be seeing you again, Isabella," that creep's voice whispers in my ear.

"Fucking hell," I groan.

He walks shoulder to shoulder with me, bumping into me every few steps. "You're still doing the escort thing, right?" When I step away he grabs my ass.

"Oh, fuck off!"

He scowls. "You know I'm your superior, right?"

"I don't report to you."

"You will tonight. So if I order you to polish my rifle—"

I gag dramatically. "Are we fighting side by side on this operation?"

"Possibly. I'll be offsite for a side mission but then I'll be on standby waiting to move in when needed. And you'll be providing support for those going in to capture President Lewis."

"You might wanna sit this one out. My aim's been a bit off." I glare at him. "It'd be a real shame if you were a victim of friendly fire …"

"Oh, I missed your feisty ass. And I'll risk a fragging if need be. This is a mission I have to take."

"Any particular reason why?"

"I think that sonofabitch Johnson will come out of hiding for this one," Stevenson says, "and I want to be the one to confront him."

"Dion's been MIA for two years. What makes you think he'll show?"

He smirks. "Let's just say we have something he wants. It may not be tonight, but he'll definitely turn up sooner or later."

"And what happens if you come across him or your former Renegades or whatever you call them?"

"Our orders are to capture Dion Johnson … If he and I cross paths, I might be able to get him to drop his guard. As for everyone else, if I can't capture them or convince them to defect to the winning team, I guess I'll have to put 'em down."

I mime raising a glass. "Here's hoping they put you down instead." I smile, slipping into the crowd and leaving him behind as we climb the stairs.

We gather in a large auditorium and take a seat. Pixie and I sit in the dead center. Dozer and Elsa head up to the front of the room to join the panel of those who are in charge of this op. Don Chambers and Stevenson stand on the right side of the stage. A pasty girl with long white hair appears from the right and slides to the podium. The hood of her white leather trench coat is draped over her head but the contrast of the black lipstick and raccoon-like eyeshadow against her skin is still noticeable as hell. She's the girl I saw back at Iceworm, the one they call Ghost. She's a brilliant fighter, and a deadly scientist, second in line for the throne after General O'Brian. And she's as ruthless as an abused pit bull. One day back at Iceworm, she bit out her training partner's throat just because he wasn't enough of a challenge.

"Silence," she says. The room falls quiet.

The projector screen goes from the words OPERATION OMEGA ANAX to a map of Williamsburg, Virginia. "According to our intel, Marine One will depart from the Executive Complex just after midnight," Ghost begins, speaking in a dry, monotonic voice. "Our stealth drone will ground them here. Then a quick reaction force will drive them to this hotel where they have a government safe house set up on the seventh floor. Our latest stealth helicopter will make sure their air support doesn't reach the hotel."

After the briefing, we dressed in our Decider uniforms, armed up, and headed to the tinted civilian vehicles we'll be using. It doesn't matter if we're caught now—everything is in motion. Hell, Echelon is so confident we won't fail, our identities have all been reinstated.

Dozer walks up beside me and places a hand on my shoulder. "You ready, Izzy?"

"Hell yeah!" I reply.

"Good girl. Between you and me, all that demoralizing shit you had to do over the last year didn't go unnoticed. And if you kick ass today, and we accomplish our mission, that recommendation I put in for your promotion will get approved and you will get peppered before the Reclamation kicks off."

"Holy shit!" I shout. "Are you serious? I'm going to be a Loyal?"

"Dead serious."

September 10

Just as Corvus and Corax told us, President Lewis departed from the Executive Complex seconds after midnight. He's needed alive, so thankfully his pilot stuck the crash landing and the president survived. The Secret Service agents and USAW soldiers of the security detail who survived are currently moving through Williamsburg in undercover vehicles toward the hotel. One team is on the ground level across the street waiting to strike. My team is in one of the stealth Specter helicopters waiting to descend. We watch the presidential convoy pulling into the hotel garage on the drone footage streaming to our Gauntlets. When the civilians start evacuating out of the hotel, Ghost gives the signal to move.

The helicopter touches down on the roof the moment our ground forces secure the perimeter. USAW soldiers appear on the roof only to get gunned down seconds later. Dozer, Ghost, Elsa, Owen, three other Loyals from Ghost's unit, me and seven other Enforcers breach through the roof entrance, leaving six other Enforcers to hold down the roof.

Ghost and Dozer are in some impenetrable liquid Deva armor so they take point and wreck the sentries guarding the stairwell and the hallway where the saferoom suite is located. It also helps that they can see through walls with their Farsight Devas and get the jump on the enemies who think they have great hiding places. Thanks to Ghost and Dozer, our enemies are having a really shitty day.

"Be advised," Dozer announces, "Corvus has just informed us that a team of USAW soldiers led by a special forces group codenamed the Seraphs has been deployed. There is also a ninety percent chance Dion Johnson is with them. Our Specter helicopters will let them enter the fray just in case the target is aboard. Don't forget, we want him alive!"

Why the hell would we want him alive? I've asked that question several times and no one has told me why.

We secure the ground level and work to fend off SWAT and police who have finally arrived. A small group from the ground team branches off and makes their way up toward us. Despite our advantages, it still takes a little over a half an hour for Ghost's group to fight their way down to the seventh floor. Once they do, we storm the eighth floor so we can flank the group defending the target.

As I follow Owen, word comes in from Corvus that a USAW team has engaged our ground-floor units. Another group was dropped off on the rooftops across the street and a third landed on the hotel roof. From the sound of it, there are a lot more of them than there are of us. I'm not really sure how we're getting out of here.

One by one, friendly blips on the Gauntlet's screen vanish below and above us. A swarm of red blips takes their places. The lights go out as I down a Secret Service agent. By the time I duck into a room to reload, the backup lights kick on. A friendly grenade goes off and takes out three of the working lights, leaving some flickering. Dozer's team finally breaches the president's room. Not long after, he emerges with the president slung over his shoulder like he's a sack of onions.

Suddenly, Dozer turns and looks at the other end of the hall. "We've got company, Ghost!" he shouts, running toward the stairwell.

I barely see a helmeted figure in all black emerge from around the corner before Ghost turns and unleashes a storm of rounds from those automatic pistols of hers.

"Enforcers, get in those rooms and hold them off until we can clear our way out," she says.

I dart into an open room further up the hall, as do the others.

Dozer hands off his light machinegun to Dunn. "Give em hell, Kappa!"

With a nod, Dunn takes it and sprays rounds at the enemy as he moves to cover. Ghost aids him, firing accurate shots until she, Dozer, Owen, and the three Loyals disappear into the stairwell. A grenade goes off soon after. Thankfully, Owen shelters in time. The others exchange rounds with the enemy. I wait for their gunfire to stop so I can pop out and engage.

"Enemy Blackhawk inbound," the Specter copilot announces. A few seconds later, there is a massive explosion that rocks the area. "Blackhawk down. Touching down now for extraction."

"Copy that," Dozer buzzes in. "On the way out now!"

More rounds are fired in the hall. Another explosion cracks outside.

"Tim! Cruz! Get up to the eighth floor and flank these bastards!" Owen orders.

Slim Tim and Joey Cruz bolt down the hallway toward the exit.

"Grenade!" Dunn shouts, slinking into the room nearest him. After it blows, he reemerges. That's when two shots pop and he goes down, a bloody patch spreading out of the holes in his back.

"Dunn!" I cry out as the wounded USAW soldier scurries back into the room the president was in. Someone in Dozer's fireteam didn't dead-check everyone. Kappa's blip on the Gauntlet's minimap vanishes before I can run to him. Even though he's been a bit of an asshole to me since I distanced myself from him, losing him makes my heart ache.

Just as I lean out to attack, four soldiers clad in black rush down the hall. Eli and Benny go down for good. Carson Wells is tagged but quickly scurries back into his room. I duck back out of the hallway, still blind-firing around the corner.

As I reload my pistol, there are four rapid explosions outside and then the entire building rocks like a plane just dropped on it. There's a hissing sound and the sprinklers start spurting water. I glance at my Gauntlet with teary eyes just as gunshots crack off. Wells' blip disappears soon after. I don't see Tim or Cruz's either. There are nine red blips outside this room. Mine is the only friendly icon on this floor …

Fucking fuck!

A shadowy figure appears at the door and the soldier tries to slice the pie outside the room. I panic and start firing like an inexperienced nutjob until he dives out of the way. Then I start shooting at him through the wall.

There's a ceasefire so I get to looking for a way out during my reload. The only option I find is the window. *That'll have to do.* I tie off the rappelling rope I had attached to my assault pack to the bedpost, make sure it's sturdy, and then I move toward the window, shifting my aim from the left side of the door to the right.

I'm seven stories up. There's not enough rope to reach the ground level, but maybe I can breach the window of a lower level.

I open the window, kick out the screen, and begin climbing out. Another soldier bursts through the doorway, charging right at me like he's not afraid to get shot. I pull the trigger four times then jump out. Pretty sure none of my shots hit. I fall about five feet before my body swings into the side of the hotel. My heart's thudding in my chest like a piston. I'm not sure if I'm more scared to get shot or to fall to my death.

I hear another gunshot from above. Then the rope suddenly has some give and I drop a few more inches. The rope then gets taut and stops falling.

"Fuck!" I cry out, almost dropping my pistol. That bastard shot my rope!

I look down to see how far I am from the next floor— nowhere near it. Then I look up right as the soldier sticks his helmeted head out of the window.

"Drop your weapon and I'll pull you up," he says, as calm as if he's ordering a coffee.

I take aim. "Let go! I'll die before I let you capture me."

I yelp as the rope drops again then stops suddenly. A second figure appears at the window and fires a single round that rips through my right bicep. The pain forces my arm to drop and my pistol falls to the pavement below. They start hoisting me up. Only horrible things await me above, like torture worse than what I experienced in training ... and probably death after that. As I draw closer to the window, I draw my knife from the sheath on my chest rig. I'm not sure if I want to cut the rope and fall to my doom or if I want to stab them when they pull me in.

The desire to live becomes evident when I'm inches from them and I haven't cut the rope yet. *Elsa and Dozer will come for me,* I think to myself. If I'm caught, there's a chance I can be rescued. If I die, that's it.

They left you to die, a bitchier version of my voice taunts. *They aren't coming back for a used-up whore who served her purpose.*

When I reach the window, the guy grabs me under the arms and pulls me in. As I'm yanked inside, I thrust the knife at him. It's a dumb idea considering I'd have to somehow kill eight more Special Forces soldiers if I actually did manage to shank him. The bastard effortlessly evades my attack, grabs my wrist, and slams me to the floor, pinning my arm behind my back. Surprisingly, he's less rough with me than the cops who arrested me way back when.

"All clear, Archangel!" another USAW soldier shouts from the doorway. "Patterson's hurt bad. Gotta move!"

"Copy. We're coming!" Archangel, the guy who pulled me inside, responds.

Another dude starts binding my wrists. I writhe and squirm, cussing as I try to break free. Archangel examines me. Then he grabs my arm and inspects my Gauntlet.

"How do I take this off?" he asks.

"You can't," I spit. "But even if you could, it'd just be disabled."

The guy who cuffed me forces me onto my feet. Now Archangel stands face to face with me, looking me over through a visor I can barely see through. The other soldiers in black leave the room.

"Capturing me is a waste, *Archangel*," I say. "I know nothing. Only the Loyals know where they're takin' your president."

"Everyone knows something, Jezebel," Archangel says. "And what you know is how to operate that device on your wrist."

I scowl. "Once my people clear the AO, their Gauntlets will stop transmitting location data. And once they realize I'm still here, they'll consider me a liability and remote wipe mine."

"So we'll have to get to your extraction team before then," he says, shoving me toward the door.

I'm not going to let that happen, I think, subtly reaching for the power button on the side of the Gauntlet. All I have to do is hold it down for five seconds and it will wipe itself and shut down.

The female soldier suddenly looks in my direction. She knocks off my helmet and cracks the butt of her rifle into the back of my head. As I fall, there's throbbing pain and then blackness.

THE END

Jezebel's Story Continues In *ANGELS OF WAR: TALION*

ACKNOWLEDGMENTS

Dad, you know I had to thank you first. I couldn't have done any of this without you in my corner. And even though you are no longer with us, Mom, thanks for all of your love and support over the years. It's because of you I have made it this far as an author.

Once again, I'd like to thank my editor, Geoff Smith, for helping me cut the fluff and for making *Jezebel: An Angels of War Novella* the best version of itself. And to my cover designer, Hampton Lamoureux, you have done a stellar job with this cover. Thanks for all of your hard work, sir. I'm looking forward to more collaborations in the future.

Big shout out to my superfans and friends: Blake Herring, Katie Reeb, and Karen Baney! I put in work to get this one out in under a year for you all [and for all of the new voracious readers who've been buying *Veritas* copies and binging on Kindle Unlimited]. To my friends who have become family: Steven Lee, Crystal Laygo, Joe Blake and the Blakes [Big Joe, Cindy, Tom & Lauren], Cullen Laygo and the Laygos, James Tribie, Michelle Persaud, Tom 'Big T' Valek, Steven Han, Matt and Steph Holdorf, Chris and Ashley Solloway, Kalan Christenson, Sung Gim, Ashley Stacharowski—thanks again to you all [and to the rest of my amazing friends who have grabbed a copy] for the overwhelming support and for being there for me when it mattered most!

And to my amazing family members: Delshe´, Debbie, Donna, Crystal M., Aunt Edy, Uncle Jerry, Uncle Alan, Tamika, Nichelle, Aliah, Alan, Cathy, Rachel, Adam, Michann, and the rest of my dope cousins and relatives—thanks for all of the love and support. I couldn't have done it without any of you.

Of course, a big thanks goes out again to the hundreds of awesome readers who purchased/read *Angels of War: Veritas* since its release! I don't write for a market, I write what I love in hopes that others will love it too. That being said, you all continually give me the inspiration to keep grinding so I can get this series done quickly and not leave you waiting for more. And thanks to all of the readers who have already read *Angels of War Talion* too! If you enjoyed this novella as much as book one, please leave a review on Amazon. It would mean a lot to me and it will also help increase visibility so more readers can experience the *Angels of War* Universe. If this one gets the kind of support *Veritas* got, I will gladly write more novellas. I've already got plans for Ghost, Anne Buckingham, and Richard Thomas in the works, but feel free to tweet at me (@TheDJThompson) and let me know which character you'd like to see a side story about!

There is still more to come for Isabella in the *Angels of War* saga so please make sure you give *Angels of War: Talion* a read too [if you haven't yet] to find out what happens to this foul-mouthed weapon of mass seduction … And get ready. The end game for society and for humanity will be actualized in *Angels of War: Terminus*!

JOIN THE
MASTERLESS TRIBE